THE FOURTH LEVEL

UNDERWORLD

BOOK TWO

NICHOLAS HUNTLEY

This book is a work of fiction. Any reference to historical events, real people, or real places is used fictitiously.

First Edition, August 2017

nichhuntley.ca

WHITEWOLF PUBLISHING

Paperback ISBN 978-0-9952494-6-2

Digital ISBN 978-0-9952494-7-9

The text of this book is set in Times New Roman.

“There is nothing I would not do for those who are really my friends. I have no notion of loving by halves, it is not my nature.”

– Jane Austen

Act 1, Scene 1

The grandfather clock ticked and its pendulum swung back and forth. The second-hand span around every minute and the minute-hand ticked ever closer to the top of the dial. The blinds were shut at either side of the room, preventing light from drifting into Charlemagne's study. Various portraits and paintings were hung on the brown walls. Bubbles arose from the fish tank on the opposite side of the room, where an assortment of freshwater fishes sat around. Next to the fish tank was a bookcase with various books, and on the opposite-side a glass cabinet with more space for books beneath and inside. Next to the cabinet was a fireplace with a large mirror overtop. Next to this fireplace was the same dark brown wooden clock that continued to tick.

In the middle of the room was a long table taken from the dining room and sat in the middle. Four chairs were positioned on either side with a main chair in the back and another in the front. On one side of the table sat men in black suits and on the other, men in pinstriped blue suits with their fedoras before them. The men in the blue suits had tanned and olive skin with dark hair over the ones across with paler skin and an assortment of hair colors. At the head of the table, in front of the desk, was a man in his traditional grey three-piece pinstripe suit with his hands together atop of the table while across from the table was another man in a blue pinstripe suit, but with a younger complexion, black beard and brown eyes. He had tanned olive skin and looked to be in his late twenties. He didn't wear the suit blazer but had suspenders and a white pinstripe collar-shirt. The holsters of his suspenders were empty. The man in the grey suit had pale skin and light grey hair atop his head and moustache. His eyes were light blue and he was in his mid-fifties. In the room there were two additional men in the corners of the room with firearms at their belts and bullet proof vests overtop their blazers.

At the top of the hour, the grandfather clock chimed and the men at the table stood up.

"Very well, our time is up," the man in the grey suit said to them in an English accent.

"So it is," the man at the opposite-side of the table said.

"Since we were unable to arrive at an agreement, I'm afraid we will have to resume the pending charges on Giovanni and his affiliates for what has occurred," the man in the grey suit said.

"In which case, we will see each other again in court," the bearded man in the blue suit replied. "Good day, Mr. Cabernet."

The man left and those dressed like him left behind him. Charlemagne de la Cabernet and his attorneys remained in the room. He watched as the members of the Medici family left before looking over to his attorneys, all of whom looked at him for direction.

"You are all dismissed," Charlemagne said to them.

The men nodded and quietly left the room. Charlemagne sat back down in his chair at a slouch as he exhaled before looking to the side.

The quiet and elegant tune of a piano echoed in the library and the crystal chandelier that hung from the ceiling of Cabernet library glistened as the light from the sun refracted through to beam as bright as stars in a clear night sky. In front of the wide window of the library were open books and empty coffee mugs atop the table between the two loveseats.

The manor library always had a simple, yet formal appearance met with its (momentarily) conservative size. The shelves had yet to recover from the firesale of hundreds upon hundreds of books that were sold. Old Cabernet family portraits and an assortment of landscape paintings were hung on whatever exposed wall there was to offer. At the end of the rows of bookcases were glass display cases atop plain black stands with red velvet lining inside. They were as empty as the shelves still were. Alas, the room had received a better treatment and was on a well path to recovery.

Along the shelves, according to each small bronze plaque at the side, were used books separated from fiction and non-fiction, natural sciences from the humanities, and such. An old chessboard picked up from a yard sale could be found on the furthest wall with a window looking south. The board was placed on a small table and its pieces were amess from the last match played little over a day ago or so. Along the wall opposite the grand window, standing on a stool ladder and reaching upwards for yet another book was Tristan Merrick, spending his late-August afternoon doing some light reading.

Tristan had a calm look on his face as he held a book in his hands and ran his hand through his sweaty strawberry-blonde hair. He was dressed for the season with his brown shorts and white t-shirt that exposed the light-coloured hairs and his tanned skin. He looked behind him as a line of men left Charlemagne's study before another group of four people left behind them. The sound of cars starting in the driving was heard, and their shadows could be seen projecting into the room. Tristan got off from the ladder and began to make his way back to the centre of the library as he looked through his jade green eyes and into the open book in his hands until the door to his left opened as Diana Cambridge walked in with a plain expression.

Diana looked much as she did since last month, but with longer, but still medium-length, dark brown-black hair. She wore her favourite denim jacket around her shoulders and over a white tank top to go with her pale blue jeans and tennis shoes.

Despite her resistance in the two months prior, she had become accustomed to living under the roof of and obeying her new guardian. The exact room she stood in was a good enough reason to remain with the troves of books she'd get to absorb, novel after novel, where she could lie down in one of the loveseats and escape without a worry in the world. She held her latest novel in her hands as she looked over to Tristan. He looked at her in hopes of news about the lack of sound upstairs from the present renovations in the north wing.

"I'll take it by the lack of sound that the workers are done?" Tristan asked.

"Come and see for yourself," Diana replied, leaving out the room for Tristan to follow.

Tristan dropped his book onto the couch and began to make his way upstairs through the grand foyer. The two stopped atop the stairs and moved aside as workers moved out with the last of their equipment. The pair then walked into the hallway.

Tristan came to the door of his bedroom and looked inside the former and renovated storage closet. Diana followed by for them to look in together. The horrible and raw hardwood flooring had been replaced with the same parquet floor in Diana's room. The walls had been painted into an olive green. New windows had been added to the back with a view of the causeway leading to the garage. On the far left was a door leading into the adjacent empty room behind the side of the attic of the stables and to the far right was a patio door going to a small balcony that connected the makeshift laboratory with his room. The windows were open and letting in a nice summer breeze.

Charlemagne arrived to join them in the lobby of the north wing. He looked into the room behind them and gazed his light blue eyes around the refurbished bedroom.

“I’m sorry this took so long,” Charlemagne said. “I have no excuse for having this take so long, but at least you’ll be able to move out of the spare bedroom.”

“It’s alright. This is perfect,” Tristan replied, walking in.

“What’s going to happen to the ‘isolation chamber’ next doors?” Diana asked in reference to the empty and depressing room between Tristan’s bedroom and the bathroom.

“Well, I don’t know,” Charlemagne replied. “I thought about having my stores in there since it seemed more appropriate, but the problem is that there are just too many things that I simply shouldn’t be storing in a side of the wing that you two will be sleeping in, so I don’t think I will. For now, perhaps, we just leave it be unless either of you have a better idea.”

“Maybe you could turn it into Tristan’s own bathroom...” Diana suggested. “So he won’t have to enter mine...”

“Perhaps,” Charlemagne replied, “but the piping may prove to be an obstacle. Regardless, now that your bedroom is finished, we can bring in the furniture and make this room more of a home. I’ll help you with the bed after supper.”

“Sounds good,” Tristan said. “We’ll have to put in a pin in that bathroom idea – I don’t know how I feel about sharing a bathroom with the house brat...”

“Screw you,” Diana barked back at him.

“Diana?” Charlemagne questioned, looking to her.

“Yeah?” she replied.

“Are you alright with Tristan sharing the bathroom (at least for now),” Charlemagne asked.

Diana grunted as she thought, but there wasn’t any other option at this point. The room had also been renovated in the last month and part of the new addition were locks on either side of both doors.

“Just remember to lock and unlock the doors,” Diana sighed.

“Hey, I’m not as excited about this as you are,” Tristan replied.

“Very well, I’ll leave you to moving your things while I go work on supper...”

“Sure thing,” Tristan replied, looking over to Charlemagne as he left.

“Another day, another dinner,” Diana remarked with unease.

“Why do you say it like that?” Tristan questioned, turning to her. “You’re free to learn to cook if you don’t like his cooking.”

“Shut up,” Diana replied, walking off.

Tristan watched her go back to her room before he went to the opposite wing, past Charlemagne’s bedroom and down to the end of the hall to enter a small bedroom near the master bedroom. The walls were pink in this room and the floor was a softer brown, almost beige shade of floorboard. It was simply put together with a mere bed and night table at the side. Tristan retrieved his luggage and things from the bathroom before moving them to his bedroom in the north wing. He left his luggage in the corner of his bedroom and brought his bathroom utensils into the shared bathroom, entering from the room between his and the bathroom.

Diana’s bathroom had pristine, new black porcelain tiles and two new white sinks against a large mirror placed along the wall. The corner tub was removed and refitted with a newer model. The walls were half grey tiles and the rest a painted white. The lights had been redone with LED lights that lit the room up nice and bright. On the furthest corner was a raised section closed off by transparent glass walls and a glass door leading into the white-tiled shower. Next to the shower on the furthest wall were two slim, but tall black lockers.

Tristan claimed one of the sinks with his toothbrush before leaving to enter the empty room next door. He looked around and felt a chill in the room. There were no windows. It would have been pitch black had there not been light pouring in from either room. Tristan looked around the large room for a moment as he thought to himself and then left as heard noise coming from inside his bedroom.

•

Later that evening, Diana walked into the kitchen as Tristan was rinsing the dishes in the sink after dinner. Diana froze for a moment as she realized Tristan's presence. Tristan's ear twitched as he realized her presence. She took a step back and moved to leave as Tristan turned to her.

"Can you help?" Tristan questioned.

"Sorry?" Diana questioned, looking over.

"Can you load the dishes?" Tristan asked. "Or if you want, can you rinse, and I load?"

"Sure," Diana calmly replied, walking over.

"This goes twice as fast with help," Tristan remarked as he moved over to the dishwasher.

"That's usually how it works," Diana awkwardly replied as she came to the sink.

Diana rolled up her sleeves and turned on the faucet. She began to rinse the dishes before handing them to Tristan.

"Aren't you a saint anyhow," Diana remarked to him. "Doing the dishes and cleaning up the kitchen."

"I just like to play my part in the house," Tristan replied.

Diana didn't reply. Tristan looked at her reaction as she seemed annoyed at him somehow.

"Anyways," he added, taking the next dish. "Do you know what I want to do?"

"What?" Diana questioned, handing him the last of three dinner plates.

"I want to turn that creepy room into a personal gym. We could get some mirrors installed along the wall like in the bathroom, and we could get some weight machines, dumbbell racks and even maybe a treadmill."

"Why a personal gym though? Why don't you just go out to one like everybody else?"

"They don't let you in if you're under eighteen... also, the purpose of having a *personal* gym is that it's *personal*."

"I see," Diana replied, turning back to the sink as she looked down at the pot inside. "Don't you want to do that kind of thing with Peter or Aaron?" she asked in reference to Tristan's friends.

"Peter has his own. I don't know about Aaron though," Tristan replied, watching Diana's hands as she rinsed and washed the pot without soap.

"Okay. So... you want a personal gym, and?"

Tristan grew silent and shy as she continued to wash the pot with difficulty.

"And," Tristan replied, moving around the dishwasher lid to stand at the sink next to Diana. "Here," he added, picking up a dish towel and adding some dish soap with it. "You need to get the grease with this because water is insolvent with it and you'll never get it clean."

Diana took the dishrag and proceeded to clean with an embarrassed tone as she avoided looking at Tristan.

"And?" she questioned.

"And, well... if we're going to turn the room into *something* then it'd be only fair to get your approval. Especially since you're not too happy about sharing the bathroom with me, and if we turn that room into a gym then I'll still be sharing the bathroom with you."

"Oh," Diana responded, washing the soap off the pot before handing it to Tristan.

Tristan took the pot and placed it on the drying rack next to the sink. Diana then began to wash a glass oven dish.

"Do whatever you want then," Diana replied.

"And, you know, you'd be free to use the gym too. It wouldn't just be mine," Tristan said. "If you want..."

"Okay."

"I mean, it would even be cool if we could, I don't know, work out together. It could be more fun for the both of us."

"Right," Diana replied, looking over to him as she turned off tap and put the glass oven dish on the drying rack. "I mean, I kinda use the library all to myself."

"No, you don't," Tristan denied. "I'm in there about as much as you. This could be a bonding experience."

"Bonding experience? Why do we need to bond?"

"What do you mean?" Tristan questioned, feeling a little disheartened.

"I didn't think you – we're not exactly friends. We're roommates."

Tristan didn't reply and thought to himself for a moment as he looked over to Diana. Diana did the same before she decided it was time to leave.

"Do you think that I don't like you?" Tristan asked as she was about to leave.

Diana didn't reply.

"Because I do like you," Tristan answered.

Diana turned the knob to leave as she turned her back on him again.

"I mean, I like you as a person of course," Tristan clarified. "Not like you, as in, I *like* you. I – I'll just shut up."

Diana smiled and turned to him.

“Relax,” she said with a smirk. “I get it.”

“I just thought that you thought that I didn’t like you,” Tristan explained.

“I didn’t.”

“Forget I said anything then,” Tristan replied, sighing as he began to feel flushed and embarrassed.

Tristan walked over to her and together they left.

“It’s okay,” she said as they walked side-by-side. “You... you get that gym set-up if you want.”

“Okay,” Tristan replied.

The two of them made it to the grand foyer, but before Tristan could go back to the library, Diana stopped at the foot of the right staircase to look over to him.

“Where are you going?” Diana asked. “We might find some weights downstairs in the cellar.”

“What?” Tristan questioned. “You think so?”

“Yeah, why not?”

“I think whatever we *do* find downstairs, it’ll be a little outdated, don’t you think?”

“Just because the equipment is old doesn’t mean it can’t still serve a purpose, right? People have been working out for decades, even centuries. We could take a look.”

“I guess,” Tristan replied, turning around and walking over to her.

The two of them made their way back to the kitchen and into the corridor that led to the freight elevator that went down to the garage. Tristan hit the switch to call the elevator, and the wide doors of the lift slid open. Tristan and Diana entered walked in before hitting the button to go down. From the corridor outside the elevator, they turned right instead of left to continue down the corridor and reached a set of double doors. Tristan opened and held the door for Diana to enter first.

The structural beams for the house were low and an array of different shapes could be seen hidden underneath white sheets ahead. In the closest section, large barrels, a thick freezer door, and many storage containers could be seen around. The unpolished, grey floorboards around was like the original floorboards underneath Tristan's new floorboards.

Tristan found a string along the ceiling and pulled it as he joined Diana. A bit of light did little to compliment the musty cellar with the sunset pouring in through various small windows along the top of the right wall.

Diana began to scavenge around with the expectation of finding a dusty old machine somewhere whilst Tristan did little in hopes for any equipment. Instead, he began to go through the furniture.

Tristan pulled the sheets off a smooth oak desk that he found. The desk stood beautifully on its four legs and it had a smooth surface. It had three drawers with the middle being extremely slim. He examined the desk and began to move it around before retiring the idea of bringing it up. Meanwhile, Diana had found boxes labeled 'Halloween decorations' and began to open each one with mild excitement.

Inside, she found a bunch of jars with preserved 'fake' organs, some old books that were falling apart, some unlabeled bottles, and some skeletons and detached skulls. Diana shoved the box aside as she found a different box with portraits of daunting figures.

Diana quickly jerked her head around as she heard the creak of the cellar door open behind them.

"What are you two doing down here?" Charlemagne asked in curiosity, walking inside. "Oh dear, I almost forgot about all this rubbage. How did either of you find this place?"

"I found it a couple of months ago," Diana answered.

"We were looking for some weightlifting equipment but couldn't find any," Tristan mulled, running his hand over his newfound desk. "I did find *something* though."

"Oh, is that right?" Charlemagne asked as he looked at the desk behind Tristan. "It appears you've found my old desk."

"Your old desk?" Tristan questioned

"Yes. Have you taken a fancy to it?"

"Yeah, I was thinking about putting it in my room since we haven't bought one yet... but there's just one down-side to this desk."

"What's that?" Charlemagne asked, placing his hand over his old desk.

"The side drawers each have these golden handles, but the middle drawer doesn't. I can't seem to open it either... there's this keyhole too. Do you still have the key?"

"There is no key," Charlemagne explained. "It's not a drawer. Look."

Charlemagne brought both hands under the middle of the desk's surface and lifted it up to reveal a secret compartment in the middle. Charlemagne quickly closed the compartment as he looked over to Diana who had her back turned.

"You see," Charlemagne remarked.

"Oh..." Tristan replied.

Charlemagne turned to Diana and walked over to her.

"Seems to be too early for Halloween, I'm afraid," Charlemagne jestered.

"Tell that to the stores in town," Diana replied, putting away a box where she had found as skeleton with a noose around its neck.

"Now wait a minute," Charlemagne remarked with realization, squatting down as he opened the box. "I don't remember this decoration..."

"Very funny," Diana replied.

"Well," Charlemagne said, closing the box and standing up, "I suppose there's no fooling you. The same joke worked on my sister when we were kids.

Charlemagne turned back to Tristan as he began to move the desk, causing the feet of the desk to rub with the floor and make a terrible noise.

"Hold on there, Tristan," Charlemagne said. "I'll help you in a minute."

"I'd love to get to decorate this place for Halloween," Diana remarked, stacking the various boxes she had found and turning to Tristan as Charlemagne walked over to him.

"You sound just like my sister," Charlemagne said. "Allodia loved to decorate the manor every Halloween. It's her favourite holiday- I'm sure of it. She made the rule that we would never throw a Halloween party without her. She loved to plan them. However, that didn't last..."

"Why?" Diana asked as Charlemagne lifted one side and Tristan lifted the other of the desk.

"She left of course. She went to university and celebrated her Halloweens there instead of here. She never came back to live in the manor after that..."

"Oh..." Diana replied as she followed the men out of the basement. "So, I take it there's no antique weightlifting equipment then."

"I'm afraid not. There used to be – it was indeed 'antique' stuff, and I sold it all off back when I was... you know, planning on liquidating the Cabernet assets. Alas, you'd be better off with some newer equipment if you'd like. Although, what were your plans?"

"I thought we could turn the room next to mine into something useful, and I decided a gym could be useful... for the both of us, you know," Tristan said. "I was thinking about getting some good lighting, some mirrors on the wall and some flooring. All of that and make that room less eerie than it is."

"Oh, well, if you both think this would be a good idea then I approve," Charlemagne replied. "Just send me an email about this and I'll sort it out in the morning."

"Sure thing," Tristan replied as they rested the desk in the elevator. "Thanks a lot."

"No problem," Charlemagne replied as Diana pressed the button to go up. "I was surprised by this idea and I'm quite fond of it. It's important for youth your age to stay fit and I'm glad you have enthusiasm for this."

Act 1, Scene 2

Tristan looked at his desk as he continued to wipe it down with a towel and some wood polish. He placed his hands underneath the middle of the surface and lifted it up to reveal the secret compartment. He ran the towel through to give it a good clean. He then quickly closed it as he heard some footsteps pass by outside. Tristan jerked his head to look behind and saw nobody pass. He then looked back at his desk and pushed in his chair before stepping out of his room to return the cleaning supplies to the boiler room.

The boiler room was a wide room downstairs in the north wing of the house, but disconnected from any corridor or doorway inside as the only way to get in was through the back patio. Technically, the room was next to the Charlemagne's study, but since it was a maintenance room, it served no purpose having its entrance in his private room. The room itself held various pipes, machinery, a back-up power generator and batteries as well as the residence laundry machines.

Tristan put the wood polish back where he found it on a shelf above the dryer and threw the rag into a hamper next to the washer. He then exited the room and looked over the quiet waters of the pool under the moonlight. He then went inside and made his way to the library where he found Diana lying on the loveseat with her face into the book she had been reading for the last two days.

Diana barely paid attention to him and didn't bat an eye as she kept reading. Tristan looked at the mess she had made on the floor with the various different books scattered about. They had recently been at a yard sale and Diana picked up various novels for her to consume in the last days of summer now that she was almost finished her summer schooling. He sighed as he walked over and started to pick them up one by one. Diana lowered her book from her eyesight and looked over to Tristan in front of her.

"Excuse me," she said.

"Yes, you're excused," Tristan replied. "Look at this mess."

Tristan arranged all the books onto the coffee table before he took his own book and picked up the mugs.

"Where you going?" Diana asked as Tristan was about to leave.

"I'm going to bed. I'm exhausted," he replied. "You should be going to bed too. Don't you have school still?"

"Yeah," Diana replied. "You're not the boss of me though. I'll head up when I start to feel tired."

Tristan shook his head at her and left.

"What an ass," Tristan said to himself, shaking his head.

Tristan went to the kitchen to put his mug in the sink. He then went back upstairs to his room and stopped under the doorframe. He looked inside at his dark room lit by the light coming from the corridor and smiled. His bed (a double bed) was in front of him with the backboard against the wall on Tristan's left. His desk was next to the bed, which meant that it was also right next to the door going into the gym and near the window. On the wall opposite was a dresser with Tristan's luggage next to it. He had yet to unpack. Tristan walked around his bed and set his book on his desk, turned on the lamp set atop the desk and picked up his phone underneath his pillow, unplugging it from the charger connected underneath. He then proceeded to take off his grey hoodie before going over to his luggage to get the grey sweatpants he wore to bed. He then walked over to close the door to his bedroom so he could get changed.

The bathroom lights flicked on automatically as Tristan stepped inside afterwards to go wash his face and brush his teeth. He then walked back to his room, moving towards his bed, but not before looking over to the door as he heard a knock.

"Come in," Tristan said, assuming it was Charlemagne.

Charlemagne opened the door and walked in with a mug in hand.

"Goodnight, Tristan," Charlemagne wished as he gave a warm smile over to him. "I noticed the lights off and door open at the end of the hall. Is Diana still downstairs?"

"Probably," Tristan replied, opening his backpack to take out his laptop and leave it over his desk. "I swear all she ever does is read, read, and read."

"Much like you, except in a different genre. She enjoys her novels," Charlemagne defended.

"I don't read with every moment I get," Tristan replied. "I do other stuff – lots of other stuff."

"I know you do, but reading is Diana's pastime. It's a good one, might I add," Charlemagne remarked. "Don't take that away from her or discourage it."

Charlemagne paused for a moment, expecting Tristan to reply. Instead, he opened the covers to his bed and prepared to get inside.

"I'll see you in the morning. Goodnight," Charlemagne concluded.

"Yeah, goodnight," Tristan replied, watching him as he closed the door.

Tristan took a deep breath and took off his shirt. The thin gold chain necklace around his neck and amulet attached raised up into his shirt as he removed it before falling down onto his chest. Tristan threw his shirt aside and then lowered himself into his bed. He buried the side of his head into his pillow and thought for a moment as he looked out his window. He had forgotten to close the blinds. Tristan's eyes began to slowly close as he gave into his tiredness. They instantly opened as the door to the (future) gym opened with Diana marching inside.

"Jesus," Tristan remarked, moving backwards as he looked to Diana. "What the hell?!"

"What's up?" Diana questioned, walking around Tristan's bed to turn on the light in the room before lying down at the front of the bed and setting her feet atop of Tristan's opposite pillow.

"What are you doing? Get out," Tristan complained.

"No," she replied. "Look at what I found in the cellar."

Diana grinned as took out a small box in her hoodie and she shook the box of cards in her hand.

"Wow, a deck of cards," Tristan sarcastically replied. "Get out."

"Not just any deck of cards. A deck of divination cards that can predict your past, present and future."

"Oh yeah?" Tristan responded, turning onto his back and climbing up as he looked over to her with displeasure. "Did you bring a Ouija board too? We could contact the unsettled spirits of the Cabernet household."

"Funny," Diana replied, opening the pack of Tarot cards. "Come on, let me give you a reading."

"Tomorrow," Tristan sighed, lying back down and looking up.

"What if you die tomorrow? We'll never know if we don't do it now."

"I don't think that's how it works," Tristan replied. "Whatever my future is set by fate, it can't be changed, even if you know what's to come."

"That's a lame and probably incorrect outlook to life," Diana replied.

"Well, it's an outlook that lets me sleep at night unlike you."

"Alright, we're doing this," Diana said, shuffling the cards. "Past, present and future. Let's go."

"Do you even know how to read these?" Tristan asked.

"Yeah, an old gypsy woman that lived on the floor below taught me about these back when I was a kid," Diana replied as she shuffled. "Alright, pick a card."

Tristan sighed and reached over until he felt the deck of cards. He picked one out and threw it over to her.

"The tower," Diana described, looking at a card with a creepy design of a tower being shot by a bolt of lightning.

"Great..." Tristan remarked without enthusiasm. "What does that mean?"

"It means change. Perhaps your life has changed in its path and it came crashing down on you, or perhaps you had something great in the past and it's no more. Either way, the change was sudden and grand."

"Yeah, that is *so* vague," Tristan complained, rolling his eyes. "And it doesn't help that you know that my parents were killed, so you know that I have had a big change in my life."

"Shup up and pick another card for present," Diana requested, ignoring the fact that Tristan had just brought up his parents for the first time since the time they met at Salmar's house.

Tristan felt his cheeks flush and his forehead perspirated. He took a deep breath and brought himself up to sit up. He looked at Diana she held the deck of cards towards him as she laid down nearby on her side, but a bit further down. Tristan reached over and picked another card. He tossed it down, but it landed in front of them. It depicted a caricature of the Devil with red skin, horns, goat legs and wings. He sat in a throne and below him were two naked humans with chains around their necks, tied below the throne of the Devil.

"Yikes..." Tristan remarked. "What does that mean?"

"It means you're literally Satan," Diana replied, picking it up. "I'm kidding. It means enslavement... being in a state of enslavement whether it be to something material, or physically enslaved – which I doubt. It can also be figurative enslavement to something..."

"Like what?" Tristan pressed.

"I don't know..." Diana replied. "Only you could know."

"Alright, give me my last card so you can get out of here."

"Perhaps enslavement to being a jerk..." Diana muttered.

"What was that?" Tristan questioned even though he heard her.

"Nothing," Diana replied, bringing the deck over to him. "Pick a card."

Tristan picked a card as he looked at her with a frown. He looked at the image with the card in hand before tossing it onto the bed. It depicted three swords side-by-side and nothing else.

"Three swords," Diana said, looking at the card. "I, uh... don't actually know what this one means. Any of the ones with numbers, or reversed, are beyond my comprehension."

"Oh, well that's great. I didn't want to know my future anyways," Tristan replied.

"Sorry about that," Diana replied, scratching her head and taking the card back. "I'm sure it was good or something."

"Thanks."

Tristan looked over to Diana as she gave a quick look at the deck in her hands before beginning to leave.

"Hey, Diana," Tristan said, looking over to her as she was about to leave.

"Yeah?" she asked, looking to him. "What is it?"

"Goodnight," he said.

"Goodnight," she replied, opening the door and leaving.

Diana closed the door behind her and started to go off to her own room. Tristan looked at the door for a second and closed his eyes as he clenched his teeth.

"You idiot," he said to himself, throwing the covers over and getting out of bed.

Tristan closed the door into the gym, closed the blinds, and then went over to turn off the light before going to his bed. He got into the bed and sat for a moment as he looked around his room. He held an uncomfortable face as he looked at the bare walls and lack of decorations in the room. He gave a sigh and lowered himself into the covers again. He then moved over to the desk to turn off the table lamp and lie on his back to fall asleep.

Diana had returned to her room. She looked around and went to her bed to remove her hoodie and sweatpants before climbing into bed. She held a frown over her face as she closed her eyes and tried to fall asleep as well.

Act 1, Scene 3

Charlemagne turned off his computer in the lab and stood up from his stool as he took a sip from his chamomile tea. The mansion was quiet. He walked out of the lab and onto the patio that connected to Tristan's bedroom. A light wind picked up as they reached the last days of summer. Charlemagne rested his arms atop of the balusters, setting his mug down so he could put his hand in his face and move them up to rub his eyes. He then brought them down, took a deep breath and looked up to the sky with a calm smile.

Charlemagne's eyes came down to look over to the Nattau River and quiet town on the other side. He then picked up his mug and took another sip before tossing the rest over to the bushes below. Charlemagne walked into his lab and exchanged his lab coat on the table in the middle of the room so he could put the coat back where it should be. From there, he made his way to his workbench where a metallic canister sat atop. It was slightly cylindrical and transparent in the middle. Above the workbench were blueprints titled 'Plasma Canister.' He set the prototype back and decided to leave, turning off the lights behind him as he opened the door and exited the room to go across the foyer and towards the master bedroom.

The next morning, Charlemagne found himself explaining the canister to Tristan, who was still in the clothes he went to bed in.

"You see," Charlemagne explained. "Plasma is an extremely hot substance to house in any conventional storage tank. We cannot lower the temperature of these substances either. The high energy is required to sustain ionization, or loss and addition of electrons. The magnetic field of this light, new storage canister will make the work my scientists at Cabernet Tech are doing on our fusion reactor much easier. It should manage to keep plasma hot and dense for them to transport and continue to do their research."

"Have you tested this prototype out yet?" Tristan questioned.

"Oh no," Charlemagne replied, taking it from Tristan's hands. "It's not done. I was going to finish it last night but found myself to be unusually too tired to do anything else."

"Okay."

"Anyways, I just wanted to show that to you. You can go and have breakfast now. Sorry for keeping you from eating."

"No, it's okay. It sounds pretty cool," Tristan replied, opening the door to leave. "Thanks."

Charlemagne walked out of the lab with Tristan, and the two came downstairs. Charlemagne had more life in his eyes, but Tristan seemed to be sluggish. Tristan entered the living room and turned on the TV while Charlemagne went to the kitchen.

The living room had received a makeover thanks to the kids. The two sofas facing one another had been exchanged for a larger, more modern couch placed on the side closest to the foyer, and a flat screen TV on the other end.

Tristan left the living room to go to the kitchen and get something to eat.

"Oh, it appears as though we'll have another cheerful summer day, today," Charlemagne said, putting some slices of bread in the toaster. "Do you fancy some toast, Tristan?"

"No, thank you," Tristan replied, taking the milk from the fridge. "I'll just have some cereal."

"Very well," Charlemagne replied, picking up the kettle to fill it up with some water. "How about a cup of tea?"

"Uh…" Tristan hesitated. "Alright then. Yes, please."

"Very good. A cupper will wake you, my dear boy."

Tristan poured some cereal into his bowl and then took the bowl into the dining room. He sat the bowl down and began to poke at it. Charlemagne came by later with a tray carrying his toast, a plate of butter and some marmalade, and two cups of English breakfast tea on saucers.

"Here you are," Charlemagne said, handing Tristan his saucer. "Sugar is on the table. I'll fetch some cream."

Charlemagne returned with some cream in a small pitcher and set it on the table. He then moved his tray over to the opposite side of the table and sat down. He retrieved a napkin from the middle of the table and set it on his lap before he began to dig into his own breakfast. Tristan continued to poke at his cereal, which was quickly becoming soggy. The TV had begun to talk about politics as Tristan looked over to Charlemagne.

"You know, for a man with a French last name, I'm kind of curious how you ended up being so English with the accent and mannerisms."

Charlemagne laughed as he stirred and dissolve the sugar in his tea.

"I was raised in East Anglia with my grandparents when I was about three years old until my granddad passed away when I was eight," Charlemagne replied. "My parents were too young and too busy to raise me themselves. Mind you, they were still in high school when I was born and then went on to college. It was only when my mother was pregnant with Allodia (my sister) that they decided to take charge – she was born the same year that my grandfather died, so they had no choice, really. My dear grandmother was devastated by the accident that she was in no state to raise me herself. I spent the following summer in the manor until I was transferred to a boarding school in Harlech – the same boarding school where my father went and had met my mother in."

"Funny, I was raised by my grandparents for a time at their farm."

"I assume they have passed on," Charlemagne asked.

"Yeah…" Tristan replied. "I had no other family to take me in after my folks died. Well, actually, I have an aunt, but I have no idea where she is. I think she's a nun or something in the United States."

"Interesting, perhaps we could look into her…"

"To have her take care of me?"

"I actually had a visitation in mind, but it's all up to you."

"No, it's okay. I don't know her and even if we did contact her, I'd still prefer living here. Anyways, how did your folks end up in England? You didn't explain that."

"Well, it's a long and complicated history, but our business started in at small town south of Harlech a long time ago. We were French immigrants that made our way there from Britain. During the start of the last century, we pushed our operations into Harlech, which was where we really grew. During the war, my grandfather spent lots of time in England as a soldier of the Canadian Army, and he liked it there, so when it came time to retire, he chose to die there. My grandfather had the largest influence on me than anyone in my life."

"What was he like?"

"Oh, he was an eccentric figure, adventurist, explorer and such. An interesting fellow, indeed. It was a great and sudden loss when he died so suddenly…"

"How did he die?"

"A tragic car accident, I'm afraid — anyways, where's Diana?" Charlemagne questioned, bringing the napkin on his laps up as he stood up. "Doesn't she have schooling?"

"She left hours ago," Tristan replied. "It's already almost ten o'clock."

"Oh my, so it is," Charlemagne replied, looking at his Swiss watch. "I didn't realize I slept in last night."

"This just in," the newscaster in the background said in the other room.

"Why did you turn on the TV? You really shouldn't have that on if you're not going to watch," Charlemagne said, walking over to find the remote.

"I like to listen," Tristan replied.

Tristan picked up the remote and looked at the TV screen. Charlemagne paused as he looked at the image next to the news anchor displaying a mug shot of a familiar old man.

"Nero Medici, who was transferred to Allabrese Hospital earlier this week has been confirmed to have died this morning. The 82-year-old former mob boss was transferred from North Albert Penitentiary for health issues, having been sentenced for life on accounts of drug trafficking, arson, first-degree murder and various other charges… We tried to get a hold of a representative of the Medici family but were unable to get a hold of anyone. Rumours still circle Medici Construction and the fate of the current owner Giovanni Medici since his disappearance in relation to conflict between him and Charlemagne de la Cabernet last summer. His whereabouts remain unknown."

"Old Nero…" Charlemagne said, sitting down on the couch. "Bah, what crime hasn't that family committed?"

"In stranger news," the newscaster said, "Nattau County Police are currently investigating a break and entering at the home of a family of three in Allabrese. Police have yet to comment on the incident, but the family have expressed suspicion that the intruder was none other than a ghost. The mother, who has asked to remain anonymous, stated that she did not see anyone when the intrusion had occurred, but did watch as glass suddenly shattered, furniture was thrown and ripped apart – all while feeling the cold sensation of someone being nearby. Her son is currently at Allabrese Hospital for treatment of a broken wrist after being attacked by a perpetrator he was unable to describe. We'll have more after this break…"

"Ghosts?" Charlemagne questioned. "I doubt it," he scoffed, raising the remote as footage was shown of a police officer with a clear biohazard bag holding a green goo. "Curious in the least."

Charlemagne turned off the TV and rejoined Tristan in the dining room. Tristan stood up and walked to the kitchen to wash his bowl and spoon before walking back out, going upstairs to his room and checking his phone. He looked around his room and scratched his head before going to the bathroom to shower. He then got dressed, brushed his teeth, and returned downstairs to meet Charlemagne on his way out.

"I'm going into town," Charlemagne announced, looking over to Tristan. "Care to join me?"

"I think I'll stay here," Tristan replied, walking past him. "I didn't sleep well and just want to relax."

"Oh, why's that? Is it the mattress?"

"No, it wasn't the bed. I just… am a little anxious about school, that's it."

"Ah, yes. The new school year. I understand. I'll see you in a bit then."

"See you," Tristan replied, watching Charlemagne leave.

Tristan shook his head as the door closed. He then walked over to watch Charlemagne in his classic three-piece suit enter his luxurious black car. Tristan went to the library once Charlemagne had gone to sit on a couch. He looked around for a moment, deciding on what to do before standing up to go outside onto the patio. He found a lounge to lie in as he got his phone out and decided to message his friends. Tristan's mobile began to vibrate as he got the first responses.

Act 2, Scene 1

Charlemagne drove off from the manor and onto the road by the bank of the river. He made his way over the steel bridge and straight for town to pull into parking lot of the Nattau County Police building.

The N.C.P. building was a tall and wide three-story building with brick walls, white-framed windows and a green-slanted metal roof. Charlemagne looked over to the daunting structure, left his vehicle, and walked around and through the front doors.

The foyer of the police station smelt strongly of coffee and held an ambience of telephones ringing and chatter. The main counters were elegant, but this elegance was distorted by the tall and thick protective glass that separated the area to the public from the office where two officers sat. In the public space were couches in front of the windows looking out onto the streets of downtown Allabrese, and various leafed plants to add atmosphere to the room. On the right of the reception desk were reinforced double doors and an access pad leading into the rest of the station.

Charlemagne walked forward and leaned against the reception desk as one officer looked over to him from the other side of the pane.

"Mr. Cabernet," the woman said in disappointment. "How can I help you?"

"I was wondering if Sergeant Horton was in at the moment," Charlemagne asked.

"I'm afraid not," she replied. "He's on vacation."

"Oh," Charlemagne replied. "What about Chief Phillips?"

"He's currently out at the moment. What is it that you want, Mr. Cabernet?"

"Okay," Charlemagne replied, thinking for a brief moment and he stroked his chin. "I was requesting access to information on current case."

"Do you have the police file number?"

"No..."

"In what regards are you involved in this case, Mr. Cabernet."

"I'm... not involved... at least yet. I believe I could be of assistance."

"Mr. Cabernet, we've been over this," the woman said in a boring tone. "The police station will call you if we *ever* need your help. Until that day comes, I will have to insist that you leave if there is nothing more that I can do for you."

"You don't understand!" Charlemagne replied. "I need information about the B&E today. I would like to inquire about some evidence they picked up at the crime-scene. I would like to analyze it to help solve the case."

"I'm sure you'd like to. I must insist that we have a team of highly skilled forensic analysists. I doubt any evidence will leave behind anything that our teams won't be able to find."

"That's the thing though," Charlemagne explained. "They will. They're going to dismiss the gh- the true culprits and come to a simple conclusion."

"It's Occam's Razor, Mr. Cabernet."

Charlemagne backed off for a moment and tried to calm himself. He looked away and came back to the secretary.

"Okay," Charlemagne said. "If you could simply disclose which detective was in-charge of that case. I would be more than delighted."

"I'm sorry, Mr. Cabernet. I cannot disclose the contents of this police report beyond the public details."

"Damn," Charlemagne muttered. "Alright. Alright then. I'll just go then."

"It would be appreciated."

Charlemagne turned around and looked over to the man in a dark blue uniform that had just entered the building. He stopped at the main entrance as he looked at Charlemagne with a displeased look.

"Charles," the man said. "What are you doing here? What have we confiscated this time?"

"Nothing, Chief Phillips," Charlemagne replied. "How are you? I had just arrived to see you in fact."

Charlemagne stepped forward to shake the chief's hand as he continued to frown at him.

"Do you have an appointment?" Phillips questioned. "Or is this about that cheque you owe us for damages to the old mine?"

"It's certainly a matter of business," Charlemagne replied, putting an arm around the chief's neck. "Perhaps we should discuss this in your office."

"Very well," Phillips replied. "Just get your arms off me."

"Right," Charlemagne said, letting go and stepping away.

Chief Phillips led Charlemagne into the police station past the protected doors. The two then walked to an elevator and boarded it.

"Tell me at least what this is about, Charles," Phillips said as they rode the elevator.

"It's pertaining to a case you are working on. I thought I could be of use to the team here," Charlemagne said as the elevator arrived.

Phillips sighed as they got off on the third floor.

"You know I'm a busy man, Charles," Phillips remarked. "You get five minutes."

"That is all I'll need, friend."

The two entered the chief's office, which was a medium-sized room with a window looking out towards downtown Allabrese, specifically the central park in the middle of town. The chief had a desk attached to bookcases against the right wall. On the left wall were more bookcases with a glass cabinet and shelves. In front of the desk were two chairs, similarly set up like Charlemagne's study.

"Alright, your five-minutes start now," Phillips said, pulling out his chair to sit down at his desk.

"I need access to the confidential details of a recent case. The one about the ghosts."

"Ghosts?" Phillips questioned. "What ghosts?"

"The ghosts," Charlemagne repeated. "I had heard about a B&E that had occurred in the county today, which the victims insisted to have been the work of supernatural causes."

"Where the hell did you hear that?"

"Perhaps my sources aren't the most reliable – it was on the morning news."

"Fake news then, Mr. Cabernet," Phillips said.

"Perhaps," Charlemagne replied. "However, *was* there a B&E as of recent?"

"There was," Phillips replied. "Let me guess, however. You believe that the perpetrators were really phantoms. Don't you?"

"Well, I wouldn't be so quick to dismiss it without looking at the evidence first," Charlemagne replied.

"Well, we've dismissed it. The case is closed. It was nothing more than self-inflicted vandalism."

"What about the green goo?"

"Who knows," Phillips replied. "It could have been anything. Just because you see green goo doesn't mean it was ghosts. You should know better. It's what the perpetrators of that hoax want you to believe."

“So, will you be charging the family then? At least for wasting police resources?”

“No, we’ve decided to dismiss the case without any evidence to say that it was them that did it,” Phillips said, opening a carton of cigarettes as he sat behind his computer. “I’m sure we’ll try and find some DNA, but it’ll take some time. Until then, the case is more-or-less solved.”

The chief stood up as he started to try and light a cigarette. He moved away from his computer and went to look out the window.

“Alright then,” Charlemagne replied, rummaging in the pockets of his blazer. “And… what would the charges really be?”

“It would depend on how the proceeding goes,” Phillips said. “Anything serious to conspiracy to minor as mischief.”

“I see,” Charlemagne replied, eyeing a USB slot in the back of Phillip’s computer.

“Anyways,” the chief said, causing Charlemagne to quickly look at him. “That’s your five-minutes up. Anything else?”

“How’s Sabrina?” Charlemagne asked.

Phillips looked at Charlemagne with a slightly raised eyebrow before looking back out the window.

“Sabrina’s fine,” Phillips simply replied. “I couldn’t say the same about her mother. I’m certain she’s contracting late-stage dementia. She keeps claiming to see her mother – it’s a classic sign of dementia if you ask me.”

“That poor woman,” Charlemagne remarked, looking back down to Phillip’s computer as she moved his arm to insert the device into the USB slot. “Give Sabrina my condolences.”

“Yes. I’ve been insisting her to have her moved out of that large damn house, but she insists that her mother won’t agree.”

"Well, perhaps hiring a nurse to come see her would be the better course to take?"

"Too expensive," Phillips argued. "Anyways, this is none of your business. Get out of here."

"You're right. It's none of my business," Charlemagne replied, eyeing the device on the computer to ensure it was inserted correctly. "I'll just be leaving then."

"Good," Phillips replied before turning around. "Oh, and Charles."

"Yes?" Charlemagne questioned as he moved to leave.

"I'm sorry about your brother," he confessed. "I had higher expectations from Sal. I hated seeing him cuffed."

"As did I," Charlemagne replied in a solemn tone. "Thank you."

Charlemagne opened the door and stepped out. He walked over to the elevator and raised his wrist as though he was looking at his watch when in fact he was looking at a slim bracelet underneath. He tapped a button on the bracelet before raising his other wrist as the elevator door opened for him to step inside.

"Oh, and a quarter to twelve. I better go and pickup Diana."

Act 2, Scene 2

"Did you fail any of your courses again?" Moira asked Diana, fixing her glasses to get a better view of Diana's report card.

"No," Diana assured her with a light laugh. "And what do you mean again? I'll have you know that this was my first attempt, and at my first attempt I got an A in all of them."

Diana looked down at her grades and held a proud smile. She looked at the high percentages and then over to Moira as she gave a light smile at him with her red hair covering the yellow hood of her hoodie, which in itself covered the black top she was waring to match her jean shorts.

"Congratulations," Moira sarcastically replied. "You completed ninth grade just in time."

Yeah, I guess I did," Diana smiled. "What about you? How did you do in your computer science class?"

"I got a good mark," she said, hiding her report card from her.

"What mark? Tell me," Diana said, trying to move it from her. "A ninety-eight?"

"Yeah!" Moira replied, switching her gaze to the light street traffic in front of the school as they both waited along a bench outside the front of the school.

"We should go someplace and celebrate," Diana offered with hope.

"Sorry, but I can't," she replied, turning her gaze back over to Diana.

"Hey, Moira!" a young, but tall man said from the sidewalk.

The boy was clearly older than the two of them. He had pale skin, a muscular appearance through his tank top and shorts, and curly-black hair.

“I’ve got to go,” Moira said. “My dad is taking us out for the long weekend. I’ll try and message you, but if I don’t, then I guess I’ll just see you at school.”

“Yeah, no problem,” Diana replied, smiling at her as she walked off.

Diana watched as she greeted Jock, her older brother. The two started to rough-house together as one pushed other around before each arrived to a crimson SUV. Diana smiled as they fought for the front seat, and then looked around for Charlemagne. She continued to look around for a couple more minutes before the black sedan pulled up along the streets, letting Diana stand up and walk over to sit inside. Charlemagne immediately sped up and made his way back into town as Diana clipped her seatbelt in.

“How was your last day of summer school?” Charlemagne asked, looking over to Diana with a peaceful face.

“Alright, I guess,” Diana replied with her backpack between his feet and report card on top. “I got my marks today.”

“How did you do?” Charlemagne asked, looking over to him again as Diana focused her eyes ahead. “Ready for the next grade, I suppose?”

“Yeah, well, I did pretty well. I’m happy with my marks and feel ready for next week.”

“That’s good,” Charlemagne said with a smile. “How about we celebrate with some lunch.”

“Without Tristan?” Diana questioned as they pulled into the parking lot of a diner.

“It’ll be alright,” Charlemagne assured her. “I tried to reach him, but he hasn’t been responding. Anyhow, it was you that had just gone through summer school, not him.”

“He didn’t reply?”

"No. I tried calling the manor, but received no reply either," Charlemagne said, opening his car door to step out.

Diana came out from the opposite-side and looked over as Charlemagne opened the trunk to retrieve a briefcase. From the parking lot, the two of them walked together to the front entrance of the retro restaurant, which had a clear neon sign above the front entrance that read 'Trixie's Diner.'

"Heya," a middle-aged woman with peroxide hair said. "How can I help you two?"

"Table for us both, please, Trixie," Charlemagne requested as she came over to them with two menus.

"Certainly," she replied, bringing them over to a booth. "Can I get you two anything to start off? Tea? Coffee? A milkshake?"

"I'll have some coffee, please," Charlemagne said, looking at the menu. "And you, Diana?"

"I'll have some iced tea," she said. "Thanks."

"Sure thing, sweetie," the waitress replied before turning around.

Charlemagne looked at the menu before sliding it aside to make room for his briefcase. Diana watched as he opened. Inside was a large laptop fitted into the inside of the briefcase. It was a thick laptop, much larger than the one Tristan had.

Trixie returned soon with a tall glass of iced tea for Diana and a mug with coffee for Charlemagne.

"Who is this, Charles?" Trixie asked as she wiped her apron and took out a notepad. "I don't think I recognize her."

"This is my adopted daughter, my dear."

"Adopted? I didn't realize you were looking to be a father. It didn't seem to be that way years beforehand," Trixie said.

"Don't listen to her," Charlemagne said to Diana.

"I'm only teasing, sweetie," Trixie said to Diana with a smile. "Be careful though. This one is always up to mischief."

"So is this one," Charlemagne remarked, looking to Diana.

"Oh, then it's a perfect match," Trixie said. "What can I get you two?"

"I'll just have the usual," Charlemagne requested, handing her his menu.

"Alright then," Trixie replied, writing it down. "What about you, hun?"

"Uh… I'll just have a BLT sandwich please," Diana replied.

"You want fries or salad?" she asked as she took her menu.

"Fries, please," Diana replied as she smiled before leaving.

Charlemagne continued to fiddle with his computer while Diana watched from the other side.

"Oh, that Trixie," Charlemagne said as he typed into the computer. "She is a feisty minx. I'm surprised she didn't know earlier about you and Tristan. She's known for her grasp on gossip in town."

"Right," Diana replied. "So, what are we doing here?"

"We're having lunch of course," Charlemagne said, sipping his coffee as he peaked over the briefcase to look at her. "What else?"

"No, what are you doing?" Diana restated.

"I'm just on my computer," he replied, "trying to establish a connection with an RC device. I need to get some information on something I'm working on."

Charlemagne entered the passcode for his device and waited for his screen to load remote access to Chief Phillip's computer before showing another password screen to access his file. Charlemagne tabbed out to boot a separate program to bypass the password screen and get direct access to the chief's desktop computer.

"Alright, how am I going to find this address…" Charlemagne said to himself as he looked at his options on the desktop

Charlemagne opened the police files and started to scroll through recent entries.

"Alright then. According to forensics, the green substance was found to have traces of silicone…" Charlemagne muttered. "However, forensics also found traces of animal DNA and no human DNA. The reporting officer concluded that the disturbance was nothing more than theatrics. All three family members denied involvement. Both the mother and son insisted on paranormal causes."

Charlemagne looked through the various pictures taken of ruined furniture, broken windows, and a last of the boy's broken wrist. He then scrolled back to read the reporting officer's name and case number. Charlemagne took out a notepad and pen and began to write down an address.

"1136 Elmwood Crescent," Charlemagne said and wrote.

Charlemagne took his phone out and tapped the address into a navigation app to get directions from his location to the crime-scene. He then wrote down some brief notes from what he could see in the police file before terminating the connection between his laptop and Chief Phillip's computer. He then closed his briefcase and brought it next to him in the booth. Charlemagne then took his mug in hand and looked at Diana.

"Did you bring your report card?" Charlemagne asked, hoping to pick up conversation with her.

"No, it's in the car," Diana replied, looking down. "I got an A in every class."

"That's fantastic to hear," Charlemagne said with a smile.

"Thanks," Diana replied with a shy smile.

"Do you care if we go someplace after lunch here?" Charlemagne asked. "Or are you in a hurry to get back to the mansion?"

"No," Diana replied. "Why?"

"I need to make a stop," Charlemagne replied, looking past Diana as their food started to come over. "I think it could lead to my next big project."

Act 2, Scene 3

Charlemagne pulled up to the sidewalk of a small single-story rancher home in a quiet neighbourhood. He looked past Diana's window to get a better look at the scene of the crime with yellow tape strewn around and barricades set up to stop trespassers. Diana looked around the quiet house with the wind gently causing some loose tape to flutter. Charlemagne turned off the car engine before he got out of the car to go around to the trunk and retrieve a different, thicker briefcase with a smooth silver texture as opposed to the leather brown the laptop was in.

Diana looked through the rear window as Charlemagne got the briefcase before looking around as he walked towards the house. He knocked on the front door before bringing his hand to the doorknob to try and enter. Once that failed, he walked back along the path towards the sidewalk before turning right onto the grass. Diana finally left the car and walked towards Charlemagne as they both went towards the rear of the house.

"Charles… what are we doing here?" Diana asked as her guardian walked forward to the house to knock on the door.

"There was an accident at this house, and I want to investigate. The police got the case all wrong. I need to examine the crime scene myself and get it right."

"Okay… why though?

"I need to collect sample of a strange substance found at the crime scene. You see, the victims of the incident believe they were attacked by ghosts," Charlemagne explained, looking through some of the windows at the rear of the house.

"And you believe them?" Diana questioned.

"I don't disbelieve them," Charlemagne replied. "You'd be surprised at the strange and mystifying things in our world, Diana. "The first lesson I intend to pass to both you and Tristan is that to always be skeptical to everything you encounter for the first time whilst in the field."

Charlemagne came to the rear patio door into the house and began to try and open it. It was locked. He squatted down and set his briefcase down on the concrete patio to open it. From the briefcase, he retrieved a screwdriver and hair pin, which he begun to use to try and break into the door.

"Damn, I never thought I'd see you trying to break into a house, old man."

"I'm not concerned about the law," Charlemagne replied.

"Me neither," Diana replied with a smug smile.

"Let's see if I remember how to do this."

Charlemagne twisted the hair pin to straighten it out before inserting it into the lock of the patio door. He then positioned the screwdriver underneath the pin to start tapping in. He struggled to get the key pins to stay in place in the lock, and quickly grew frustrated as the lock failed to turn. Diana watched from behind, squatted down and waited patiently before standing up.

"Damn this lock," Charlemagne curses, jabbing the lock with the screwdriver in anger.

"Whoa there," Diana alerted, putting his hand on Charlemagne's shoulder. "You're doing it wrong – move over."

Charlemagne took a step back with the screwdriver and hairpin in-hand before Diana took both from him. Diana looked at the hairpin and put it in her pocket. She then took the screwdriver in-hand and began to wedge it between the lock and doorframe. Charlemagne watched from behind and crossed his arms to brace himself to wait patiently for her to finish. In a sudden second and sound of wood ripping, the door suddenly pushed back as Diana gently nudged it with her foot after breaking in.

“How did you…?” Charlemagne questioned. “I thought – wait. How do you…”

“Don’t ask,” Diana replied, walking inside to get a view of the mess in the kitchen. “Jeez, looks like a fight broke out here.”

“Where did you learn to do that?” Charlemagne questioned as he entered and closed the door behind him.

Charlemagne then turned around to get a proper view of the shattered glass and dishes along the checkered floor of the kitchen.

“My,” he remarked, walking over some of the glass and making his way into the dining room.

In the dining room, the dining table was flipped on its side with chairs stacked to form a tower that touched the ceiling.

“What did the… what did the police report say about this place?” Diana asked, rubbing her arms as she got goose bumps.

“They didn’t say it was ghosts for a start,” Charlemagne explained, taking notice of the articulate manner the chairs were stacked upon another without rhythm. “They concluded that it was all just a prank. However, that doesn’t add up to me.”

“Maybe it was a damn good prank.”

“Possibly,” Charlemagne replied, taking out a flashlight to get a better look around the darkened house.

Charlemagne walked into the living room from the dining room and found a couch ripped open with cotton batting scattered in pieces everywhere. He walked around to the front of the couch to get a better look and saw claw marks around the great big hole.

“Then again,” Charlemagne said, crouching down to pick up some cotton. “Maybe not. The fabric on this couch wasn’t cut by any sort of incision to look to be fake.”

Charlemagne stood up and turned to look at the great big hole in the middle of the living room window.

"It looks as though somebody tried to jump in," Charlemagne remarked. "Or perhaps, jump out."

Diana left the kitchen and came into the main foyer where shoes were scattered around, and some destroyed. Diana got a closer look and knelt down to pick one up.

"Ugh," Diana groaned in disgust, dropping the shoes quickly over the slimy substance that rubbed against his hands. "Gross."

"What is it?" Charlemagne questioned, walking into the foyer from the living room.

"I found some slimy substance," Diana sighed, wiping her hand off on the nearby wall and walking into the study in the next room.

Diana looked at the scene carefully and found papers to be scattered around with books open on the ground. She stepped out and made her way back to the kitchen where she found a pet door built into the patio door.

Charlemagne knelt down in the foyer and opened up his briefcase where some test tubes were stored with some swabs, a tablet device hooked up to the lab computer at home, and some more forensic tools such as an ultraviolet lamp, latex gloves, scalpels, needles, and the sort. He took a swab and began to gently collect some of the sample to place in a sealed tube. He then took another tube and began to collect as much as he could, filling it half-full. The substance was the same green goo that he saw on the TV, and it had a pungent odour attached to it. Charlemagne closed the tube and held it up to look at it closely as he pondered what it could be. The substance was translucent.

"Diana, do me a favour and wash your hands, will you?" Charlemagne requested. "We don't know what this substance could be, and we need to treat it as a biohazard."

Charlemagne put the sample into his briefcase and closed it before standing up to look into the study. Diana looked around the kitchen and walked over to the sink to wash her hands. Once she was finished, she dried her hands with a paper towel and walked back into the foyer where she found Charlemagne walking around the study.

"I find it peculiar how the family claimed to have not seen anything, and yet there is all this destruction. The possibilities are simple: either they are lying, or they are telling the truth that it was something unknown. If it was a ghost, I wonder as to why it was so violent? Where did it come from? I have many questions that need answering. There is not much evidence for me to look into, but I can start with this strange substance. I have to get to the labs at the research center to use their equipment and give this stuff a proper examination. In the meantime, I have no other purpose here."

Charlemagne looked over to Diana with a serious face before making his way over to her. Diana took a step back before following him into the kitchen.

"Have you found anything else?" Charlemagne asked, looking around the kitchen one last time.

"Nothing you haven't already seen," Diana replied. "The bedroom doors were shut and looked fine inside. The garage was clear."

"Did you wash your hands?"

"Yeah."

"Okay," Charlemagne replied, looking to the patio door. "Let's go then."

Act 2, Scene 4

Charlemagne and Diana stepped out from the house and back into the brightness of outside in the backyard. Charlemagne stopped and turned around as he watched Diana close the door behind them. The two then followed the path around the rear of the house back to the fence. Diana eyed an empty dog house in the corner of the backyard before the two of them left to cross the front lawn back to Charlemagne's car.

Charlemagne put his briefcase in the trunk of the car before coming around the front to join Diana. She stood at the passenger side of the car with her door open as she let the inside ventilate. Charlemagne went inside immediately, prompting her to join him as he started the car engine.

"So, what now?" Diana questioned as Charlemagne drove forward.

"Well, if you're not in a rush to go home, then I'm going to the Cabernet laboratories just out of town. I need to get this sample tested as soon as possible."

"I've got nothing to do," Diana replied, putting on her seatbelt as they left the neighborhood. "I can't wait to see the look on Tristan's face when I tell him you took me to the labs. He'll be so jealous."

"Oh, that reminds me..." Charlemagne said, bringing a hand from the steering wheel and into his blazer. "I forgot about him. See if he's replied to my message."

Charlemagne handed his cell phone to Diana, who took the phone and quickly checked.

"Nope -- hasn't even read them."

"How curious. Call him for me, please."

Diana did so, and the phone began to ring, projecting volume through the car speakers as the car system was connected to

Charlemagne's phone. The phone rang and rang, and no answer came. It went to voicemail.

"He must be busy. I can't imagine what he got himself up to."

"Do you think he's okay?" Diana asked.

"I found him to be a bit tired this morning. Perhaps he's gone back to bed."

"Yeah, maybe," Diana replied with doubt in her voice.

Charlemagne arrived back into downtown Allabrese, passing through to reach the freeway heading east. He drove faster the farther he got from town as the speed limit climbed and road widened as they arrived on the rolling plains east of Allabrese.

Ten minutes later, Charlemagne exited and slowed down on the exit ramp that brought him onto a dirt road. From this road, he turned right not too far ahead to continue along to a checkpoint that led into the parking lot of Cabernet Tech headquarters. Diana looked out from her window at the size of the compound. It was all surrounded by a tall barbed-wire fence that stretched along for at least a mile on either side. The parking lot was enormous and full of cars belonging to employees. The building consisted of several annexes with a glass annex on the right, central main sector that extended all the way to the left with an elegant and modern front entrance. Behind the main wing was a tall, simple brick building.

Charlemagne drove around the parking lot and continued along a causeway to the left side of the building at a slight decline, going to the rear of the brick annex where various garage doors were lined against the entire wall. Charlemagne drove into an open one, coming into the receiving garage of the building.

“What are we doing back here?” Diana questioned. “Why didn’t you park behind and go through the main door? I thought you’d have your own parking spot right at the main door or something.”

“Nonsense,” Charlemagne replied. “I have that parking spot only at Cabernet Tower and the head office in town.”

“But why are we back here?” Diana asked as Charlemagne shut off the car.

“Too high profile,” Charlemagne answered, opening the door. “I’m not supposed to be here… at least, unsupervised.”

Charlemagne left the car as Diana let out a smile and laugh. She left the car and stood at the opposite side of the car as Charlemagne walked around to the trunk. She followed, looking around the busy workmen in reflective vests. The room extended from the garage doors and went all the way back with miles of shelves holding various crates, skids, boxes, and sometimes skids and crates with other boxes.

“Why can’t you be here unsupervised?” Diana questioned with a taunting smile.

“Quiet,” Charlemagne replied as he grabbed his briefcase and closed the trunk. “Stay close to me.”

Charlemagne led Diana away from his car and towards a roll up door that led into a tall and wide corridor with smooth concrete flooring. Along the side of the corridor were more skids with boxes wrapped around in plastic. The hall bent right, led to some automatic double doors that opened as soon as the duo walked towards them, and led them into a small lobby. Another pair of double doors stood before them with windows on either side and an elevator shaft door on the other. Charlemagne took out an access card and brought it to a console on the right of the doors, causing the console to beep and shine a green light before the doors opened slowly. The two then entered the vestibule as Charlemagne tapped the button calling for the elevator.

The two waited for the elevator doors to open, letting them walk inside the modern interior of the elevator as Charlemagne walked over to tap his card again into a similar console above the elevator buttons, and then choose his destination as being the second floor. The elevator doors behind them slowly shut as Charlemagne eyed a camera in the corner of the lift.

"Come on, Charles," Diana said, standing underneath the camera for Charlemagne's eyes to drop down on. "Spill it. Why aren't you allowed to be here without *supervision*?"

"My presence here is conditional," Charlemagne said. "In a certain manner, I'm not supposed to be here at all."

"Why though?" Diana asked as she laughed. "Don't you own all of this?"

"I do," Charlemagne replied, sounding annoyed. "I'm chairman and owner of all of this, but Cabernet Industries is a public company with investors and shareholders. I made a promise that my work and research would be independent to the work and research of this lab. I am not allowed to come into this building without signing in and being supervised by a staff member, because I… I tend to have a 'tendency to be destructive,' which can harm our public image."

The elevators reached the second floor and opened to leave them in a bland hall. The two of them stepped out, and Diana followed Charlemagne right. The two of them then continued down toward a corridor with a railing looking to the corridor below and a tall window looking towards the rear lands of the territory. Diana spotted a large fenced pool with tall tanks to the right of it and platforms above. She refocused her attention on Charlemagne as they walked down the long corridor with gaps for doors leading into separate halls perpendicular.

"When I don't want to go through the tedious process set up for me, I do this," Charlemagne explained, turning at the third gap to tap his card at another proxy console. "I do try and refrain from letting this be a habit, of course. The last time I was even on this property was about a month ago."

"Seems like an unreasonable condition you put on yourself," Diana said as they walked down a smaller corridor.

At the end of the corridor was a similar door leading out. On either side of the walls in this hall were either thick windows looking into laboratories, or steel doors leading into the labs. All of the ones in this floor were unoccupied, and the lights in the individual labs shut off. Charlemagne tapped his access at the first door, causing the laboratory doors to slide open and let them in. The lights then automatically turned on as they came inside.

The room had a cyan blue sheen. The tiles were a slick and polished cyan, while the concrete arched walls were painted in a similar color with a ticker of a narrow yellow and black hazard line around the middle of the wall.

Diana looked around at the fancy gadgets and machines before quickly getting bored and retreating to a rolling chair to sit down.

"Bah, I don't care," Charlemagne replied to Diana as he began to set up. "I could care less what was going on here because I have confidence in those I hire to lead this place and the work they do. It is very rare that something of interest comes out of here – in other words, it is very rare that scientists here develop something that impressed me. Most of their work surrounds concepts and ideas I've forwarded to the Chief of Research. Take the fusion reactor downstairs for example. An old friend of mine and I conceptualized everything that they created. Speaking of that reactor, it had its first test early this morning."

"Tristan told me about that reactor. He seemed excited about it… something about sustainable energy."

"That's right. I had told him about it not too long ago as well," Charlemagne replied, opening his briefcase to retrieve the samples. "Which also reminds me – I have to finish a prototype and deliver it to Dr. Lambert when I get home. Can you close the window shutters for me?"

Diana stood up from her seat and walked over to look around for blinds.

"They don't have blinds," Diana replied.

"No, shutters," Charlemagne corrected. "Hit the button underneath the light button by the door. We're in a student laboratory, and I don't want to be seen by anyone that may pass through."

Diana found the button, pressed it, and watched as the glass dimmed to become a pitch black. She then walked back over to her chair as Charlemagne set up a machine.

"The destruction in that house intrigued me," Charlemagne confessed. "I am quickly warming to the idea of 'ghosts' being involved – that this was some sort of phantom attack."

"You're kidding, right?" Diana replied. "There's really no such thing as ghosts… right?"

"I couldn't say so for one-hundred percent certainty."

"Jeez…" she replied. "What next? Are we going to go hunting vampires and werewolves too?"

"Don't joke in such a manner," Charlemagne warned in a serious tone, taking the sample of goo out and inserting it into a machine.

"Even if it was a ghost, why now? Why are such events not more frequent? Why would this become the first confirmed and true sighting of the cultural trope of the spirit of the dead?"

“We shall see,” Charlemagne simply replied, peaking his eyes into the scope of the machine. “For now, I need to isolate the DNA in this sample so that the analysis can at least verify the species with the many samples archived.”

“You want to know if there’s any trace of human in that thing?” Diana asked, leaning back in her hair and picking up a stress ball lying around.

“That’s right,” Charlemagne agreed, affirming the machine to scan a strand of DNA before peaking back into the scope to find another strand to examine. “The forensics team the police rely upon overlooked searching for any DNA and assumed this substance to be gelatin, hence the traces of DNA, period. They didn’t, however, look to see what genome this DNA could be and whether it was human. Instead, they must have searched for any additional traces of human DNA in the form of hairs, skin, and other evidence.”

Charlemagne raised his head from the scope and found a notepad for him to write stuff down. He then turned to the console next to him and began to type.

“We will start by trying to match the DNA segments suspended in this substance with DNA unique and common among all Homo sapiens.”

The computer instantly *wurred* before displaying an ‘ERROR’ across the screen in a bright and bolded red font.

“Apparently the DNA strand I selected was incomplete,” Charlemagne said, reading the results.

Charlemagne typed into the computer before moving back to place his eyes into the scope. He looked into the higher magnification before writing some more notes, and then typing into the computer.

“Are these suspended nucleotides on their own? Did this substance cause the DNA to break part? I’m not seeing that it could have – they were like this already.”

Diana continued to roll in her chair as she grew increasingly bored. Charlemagne worked in silence with his eyes in the scope before he retreated and typed into the computer, setting the computer to *wurr* again. The two then proceeded to wait for the machine to finish, but not before long, it produced another ‘ERROR.’

Results printed from atop of the machine. Charlemagne ripped them out and read them.

“No similarities detected,” he said with a disappointed sigh. “The DNA was not human…”

Charlemagne threw the results on top of the computer as he frowned. He placed both hands on either side of his head and began to think.

“I mean… let’s be honest,” Diana said. “The odds of this being a real human ghost were slim.”

Charlemagne didn’t reply, but did raise his head up.

“Human,” Charlemagne said, typing into the computer. “I was being too specific, perhaps if I were to… widen the search.”

“Huh?”

The computer began to *wurr* again. Charlemagne let the machine work, and it worked for seconds, which turned into minutes. Various sequences of numbers dashed down the screen at an incredible pace. These minutes grouped into five and then ten.

“How long is this going to take?”

“Well, considering I set the computer to match the DNA with all samples in the Animal kingdom… I’d say a while.”

“What?”

Charlemagne had retrieved the sample from the computer in the meanwhile and had brought it to a separate station for him to analyze. He had taken various notes so far and was mystified.

"It's like mucous, this stuff. It is a substance with a load of various particles suspended within it," Charlemagne said. "It's curious."

"Fascinating," Diana replied with sarcasm, fetching Charlemagne's phone from her pocket.

Diana turned on the phone to see that there were still no messages or returned voicemails from Tristan. She frowned at this and began to send a message as Charlemagne to Tristan, asking him if he was okay. She then set off to browse the web, while at the same time, did so as though she was distracted. She eventually turned off the phone and put it away to instead raise her legs up and embrace them as she continued to wait.

Eventually, the noise of the machine slowed down, results began to print again, but this time the paper was much longer and spilled out to form a mess.

"Uh, the machine is done," Diana said, causing Charlemagne to look up and turn around.

"Oh, damn!" Charlemagne remarked, rushing over to sort through the long sheet of paper that was still printing out.

The results came to be about three meters in length, but most of what was printed was just code. Charlemagne rolled through the results before stopping towards the end. Diana watched as her guardian hovered his eyes over this section for a long minute.

"Well?" Diana asked.

"Well," Charlemagne replied, scratching his head. "The machine examined the DNA, and it deduced what species the sequence belongs to. Based on samples we have, the machine found a gene unique to the *Canis* genus and *lupus* species. To be exact, of the *familians* subspecies."

“Okay… can I get that in English?”

“It was a dog,” Charlemagne simplified.

Diana nodded before she asked, “So, what does that mean?”

Charlemagne’s eyes jerked over to Diana before going back at the paper.

“It means… I might have missed there being a pet… although, nothing of the sort was mentioned in the police report or clear to me at the time…”

“I did see a pet door… and a dog house,” Diana said.

“Then I’ve either missed something important, or…”

“Or?”

“I don’t know. I don’t want to say it – I doubt myself and am sure that I only want this to be true – for this to have been a supernatural spirit of some kind. Although, the fact that the DNA belongs to a dog has me doubt this and changes my opinion. I believe we have been let astray.”

“Can’t dogs have spirits as well? Don’t all dogs go to heaven?” Diana questioned.

Charlemagne looked at her again before he started to collect all the papers.

“This substance is no sort of ‘mucous’ or ‘saliva’ I have ever seen to come out of any animal. The particles are a cocktail of random particles ranging from water, gypsum, even dead skin cells to dirt and sand. I wish I could say I picked a bad sample to test, but… this was the only sample that was independent to itself… and on closer analysis, I did find it to be attempting to replicate on its own – or multiply.”

“What does any of that mean?”

“The damages of the house could have been conducted by a berserk dog…” Charlemagne instead said. “And most importantly of all, the family did not see the perpetrator, or so they claim. My thought now is that this was a dog, and that the family could be protecting it from being put down."

"But that doesn't explain that gunk," Diana said.

"No, it doesn't. You're right. My God," Charlemagne said, placing the results in a need pile above the machine before wrapping a hand around his forehead. "What have we come across? I'm stumped. I'm trying to be rational about this so bear with me."

Diana rubbed her arms as she stood up and said, "I think it was a ghost."

Charlemagne didn't reply, and instead began to collect all his things.

"Right, well, I think I'm done here. Let me take you home so you can rest. I need to run some more tests on this sample before I can make any sort of conclusion."

Diana nodded as Charlemagne packed his things. The two then left the lab and walked back to the elevator via the same route they previously took. Once the elevator doors closed in front of them, Charlemagne gave a long sigh.

"The DNA being incomplete when I was attempted to isolate it bothers me as another mystery," Charlemagne confessed. "I find it strange how the nucleotides appeared to either be coming together if not coming apart."

"A dog attack would make sense," Diana said, "but why the dog was so hostile is what I don't get either."

"I don't understand anything at this moment, my dear," Charlemagne replied as the rear elevator doors opened behind them. "I don't understand any of this at all."

Act 3, Scene 1

Charlemagne and Diana walked up the steps of the manor and through the front entrance. In the foyer, the two of them looked ahead, through the translucent curtains ahead from where they stood in the foyer, looking into the patio as she could see movement outside of multiple figures. They could recognize some of their voices to be Tristan and his friends. Charlemagne went ahead, towards the patio door whereas Diana decided to go upstairs and all the way to her room. She threw her backpack onto her bed and laid back-first next to it as she sank into her mattress.

Charlemagne returned from speaking with Tristan and walked up the stairs with the silver briefcase at his side. He went into his lab and closed the door behind him before setting his briefcase on the table ahead. He took out the sample from Cabernet Tech and began to carry it over to the large apparatus in the corner of the room. Charlemagne opened the tray and set the test tube inside before pushing it back in and going to the console next to him. He pressed some buttons before going over to the computer to sit down and begin the testing, but not before retrieving his lab coat from behind the door.

Diana groaned as she continued to lie on her bed. The sound of laughter and amusement coming from the patio could be heard in the silence of her room. She leaned and stood up to open her backpack, retrieving a copy of *Inferno* by Dante Alighieri and stopping to look at her door as she thought. She eventually stepped forward, left her room and walked down the corridor to come back to the foyer. She walked around the perimeter balcony and went to the second floor of the library before coming down the spiral staircase at the end to find a place in the library. The sound of laughter could still be heard from here.

Diana growled and left the room to walk over to the living room, and then dining room and kitchen. She looked around in the kitchen for a moment before moving over to the closet but entering a door that brought her into the attic of the stables.

The stables smelt strongly of hay and raw wood. It was slightly warm as well with heat radiating from every open window. She sat down, throwing her legs over the side of the open ceiling and thought for a moment as she looked around. Her eyes scanned the floor below before going ahead to the bales of hay above. She decided to stand up and go to the hay, finding an unkempt pile that allowed her to sit down in and open her book to read.

•

Charlemagne continued to work into the evening, running test after test in the confines of his six-by-nine laboratory. Tristan slowly opened the door and entered with a tray holding a plate of pizza. Charlemagne jerked his neck around before turning his body as he removed his safety glasses with a quaint smile.

"Tristan," Charlemagne greeted. "What have you got there?"

"Your dinner," Tristan replied. "I ordered pizza for us."

"Oh, thank you," Charlemagne replied as Tristan set the tray next to the open briefcase. "Have your friends all left?

"Yeah," Tristan replied. "About two hours ago. It's almost ten o'clock."

"Is it really?"

Charlemagne turned around to look at the time on his computer. It was almost a quarter to ten in the evening. Tristan eyed the contents of the briefcase, looking at a vial filled with green goo before going back to Charlemagne as he looked at him.

"Well, thank you very much for reminding me to eat, Tristan," Charlemagne said, turning his stool to the table in the middle as he slid the tray over to himself. "I've been lost in my research…"

"What are you looking at?" Tristan asked.

"Something extraordinary," Charlemagne explained. "Diana and I went to collect this substance this morning, and I have been both baffled and in awe of it. I have taken to naming it 'ectoplasm,' because it seems to something molded from the outside."

Charlemagne took his fork and knife as he started to cut into his pizza. Tristan looked at Charlemagne's hands in disbelief before smiling as he crossed his arms. Charlemagne told him about the house he and Diana went to before going to Cabernet Tech. He told him about how they had found incomplete strands of DNA belonging to a specific dog and how he had just begun to find complete strands of DNA belonging to the same dog in the form of dead skin cells and hairs.

"My initial hypothesis was that these strands of DNA were either moving apart or together with this goo aiding the process to reform the deceased dog. My latest tests have all but confirmed that. It has all left me quite stumped but also left me with a large sum of data which could prove to be of some use."

"I see…" Tristan responded.

"Anyways, have you seen Diana around? You said she was with you, but I haven't seen her at all."

"The last I saw of her was when I arrived, but that was…" Charlemagne paused to look at his watch. "Oh my… six hours ago. Well, then I can't say for certain where she may be.

Somewhere within the mansion, I assume. She knows her curfew."

"Yeah, well, I'm sure I'll find her," Tristan replied. "I just couldn't find her to tell her I ordered pizza, so she must be hungry…."

"Yes, but I'm sure she's around. Do find her for me if you can. She's like a cat by the way she's hid herself somewhere."

"Yeah," Tristan replied, backing up to leave. "I'll do that."

Tristan left the room and sighed after he shut the door behind him. He looked around the corridor and then went left towards the main foyer. He went around to the second floor of the library and came to the railing to look ahead.

The house was quiet and Tristan held a bored expression. He didn't stay at the railing for long as he went down the spiral staircase to the bottom of the library and then out into the foyer. Tristan came to the kitchen and as he entered, he quickly ran over to the island countertop where he had left the leftover pizza. The slices left for Diana, causing Tristan to smirk as he looked around.

"Cat? More like a rat," Tristan remarked to himself.

Tristan went back to the foyer and upstairs. He went down the long hallway and to the end where Diana's bedroom was. The door was left ajar. Tristan knocked on the door, causing it to open more and reveal Diana lying on her bed with an empty plate on her desk.

"What?" Diana questioned.

"Where've you been?" Tristan asked.

"What do you mean?"

"I mean, where did you go? I couldn't find you anywhere."

"Oh, meh. I've been around," Diana replied, focusing on her novel.

"Okay then," Tristan responded. "You're welcome for the pizza by the way."

"Hardly, it was kind of cold," Diana remarked.

"Well, that wouldn't have been the case had I known where you were."

Tristan gave a gentle sigh with his last remark. Diana looked over to him as neither of them said anything.

"Can I help you?" Diana asked in a rhetorical tone as Tristan stood there.

"No," Tristan replied. "I'm just... kind of bored."

Diana looked back at her book as she said," Well, that's not my problem. It's almost nine o'clock. Go do something *sciency* with Charlemagne or whatever."

Tristan frowned before walking off and back to his room. He entered it and sat down at his bed. Diana looked back to her door after Tristan had left and sighed as she had to get up and close the door. She then went back to her bed to read. Meanwhile, Tristan continued to sit at his bed, raising his feet up to rest them on the wooden frame. He had his hands in the pockets of his hoodie as he looked to the side with not just a bored expression, but an expression of loneliness.

Diana took her eyes off her book and raised them to her door, holding them there for half a minute before she sighed. She closed her book and pushed it onto her desk before turning off the light and raising the blanket over her shoulders to sleep. She left her eyes open in the darkness for minutes and minutes. Tristan took off his sweater and smelt his arms as he found himself to reek of chloramine. He then climbed into his double bed and without closing the blinds to the moonlight outside, he fell asleep.

•

Charlemagne continued to work as he examined the ectoplasm sample with every test he could run to collect as much data as possible. His frustration grew into the night to the point where he was throwing his pencil onto the table in the middle and cursing. Eventually, he would calm down as he wrote on his whiteboard when he'd reach the extent to his research.

From his research station, Charlemagne made his way to his workbench where he picked up the prototype plasma container. He opened a drawer underneath the bench and picked up some scrap paper to begin drafting a new design.

Time rolled forward for Charlemagne as he finished the blueprints for a new invention before he began to assemble it at his workbench, replacing his goggles with a welder's mask. Charlemagne put the finishing touches on the barrel of the invention before he grabbed a plasma container to attach into the device. After the item was finished, Charlemagne pushed it forward to the back of his workbench before he started to work on something else.

Charlemagne raised his eyes to look at the device. It had a large cylindrical barrel at the end of a large, round receiver where the plasma container sat in the middle. The weapon had a handle at the top of the receiver as well as the rear. The surface of the weapon was made of a chrome-like material, which gave it a slick shine. Charlemagne lowered his head again as he focused on developing a pair of thermal goggles.

After the goggles were finished, Charlemagne began to work on an additional gadget. This device was similar to the plasma container, but smaller and with a dial at the top. Charlemagne put it with the other tools and looked at them all. He then stood up and made his way into the bathroom to fetch some water in a kettle. He then set the kettle onto a hotplate by the chemistry set.

Charlemagne sat at his desk with the computer and picked up a pencil. He began to write notes in a scribble, setting a reminder for himself to contact Richard Huxley in the morning as well as some other reminders.

Sunlight began to filter into the makeshift laboratory as Charlemagne poured himself a cup of water, put a teabag in and left the lab. He returned to his bedroom where he sipped his tea whilst sitting atop of his bed before collapsing into a deep slumber for the next eight or nine hours.

Act 3, Scene 2

Several weeks had gone by since Charlemagne had visited the 'haunted' house, examined the ectoplasm and collected his data, and invented his various gadgets. Nothing else could be said to have occurred except that Charlemagne had contacted Richard Huxley, the Chief Executive Officer of Cabernet Industries, and told him to notify marketing and have some advertisements sent out throughout Allabrese in the event of another 'spiritual disturbance.'

Charlemagne sat in his study, typing an email with hesitance and distraction as he paused every so often to look aside. His eyes jumped from the computer screen as his phone dinged with a received notification – a text message. He brought his hand over to his phone and picked it up.

"Oh…" Charlemagne said as he read the message. "Oh!"

Charlemagne put his phone away immediately into his blazer and stood up. He then rushed out of his office and towards the opposite wing so he could get to the garage. Charlemagne skipped the elevator to instead climb down the ladder from the stores, and then rush to the pickup truck, which had been painted into a fresh coat of black paint and lime green decal at the sides that read, 'Cabernet Paranormal' with a hotline number underneath.

From the truck, Charlemagne went to the rear to get his gear. There, there were several hard-shell weapon cases as well as one with a 'Danger' symbol on the front. Inside one of the longer cases was the cannon developed by Charlemagne. In a smaller container were the thermal goggles, beige jumpsuit and black steel-toe boots. In another container were several special gadgets, and in the case with the danger symbol were plasma containers containing Boron-11 plasma.

Charlemagne immediately began to take off his blazer, vest, unbutton his shirt, and remove his trousers and shoes to strip to his white undershirt and boxers. He then put on the jumpsuit before putting on the boots with ease. He then zipped up the jumpsuit, took his phone from his blazer and took the keys for the pickup truck (in one of the pockets of the jumpsuit) to the driver's seat.

The truck's engine ignited as Charlemagne turned the engine on. He then activated the garage door to open and let him out. Charlemagne drove along the driveway, facing the orange evening sky and made his exit onto the road to drive towards the bridge. He took his phone from his pocket as he drove over the bridge, read the address on the alert text sent to him before tossing his phone to the side.

"1290 Wilbur Avenue," Charlemagne muttered to himself as he tried to concentrate on the road again. "1290 Wilbur Avenue."

The truck continued to roll forward as it drove on approach to downtown Allabrese before taking a left to instead come into the suburban outskirts. Within less than five minutes, he found himself at a small one-story white rancher. Charlemagne parked on the side of the road, got out of his car and ran to the back of the truck to get his chrome-encased cannon.

Charlemagne felt the weight of the weapon in his hands as he lifted it out of its case. He put his duty-belt around his waist first, loading it with his gadgets before he took a filled plasma container to load his cannon. The plasma container contained Boron-11 harvested from the fusion reactor at Cabernet Tech. It was a venomous green color. Charlemagne cocked and readied the cannon. He then put his goggles around his forehead and then picked up the cannon to go onwards and forwards as he faced the house head on.

Charlemagne walked to the front steps of the house, rang the doorbell and held his hands to his belt as he waited for someone to greet him. A couple of seconds went by before Charlemagne knocked again only for the door to slowly open as it was left ajar, leaving Charlemagne to invite himself in.

The house was dim. Charlemagne took his first steps with caution with the cannon pointed forward ahead of him. The foyer of the house had a sitting room to the left with a fireplace at the end, couch on the right of the fireplace and several elegant chairs on the left. Ahead was a table with imitation Chinese vases. To the left of this table was an exit as well as to the right where there was a French window leading into the dining room. Charlemagne quickly entered the dining room as his eyes met the scared life inside, hiding behind the turned over dining table. A middle-aged couple with their two children, a boy and a girl, were huddled behind the table.

"Charlemagne!" the mother exclaimed. "Help us!"

"That's why I'm here," Charlemagne replied, kneeling in front of them. "What's the problem? Why are you hiding?"

The woman immediately screamed as glass shattered against the window behind them. Charlemagne stood up as he felt the rustle of wind against him – a cold chill. He looked down to the exit of the dining room, down an ominous and empty corridor to see nothing.

"The ghost…" the father said with heavy breathing. "The ghost's been throwing plates at us non-stop. I tried to call the police, but they didn't take me seriously, so I called you!"

"I see," Charlemagne replied, standing up and holding his gun forward. "Your safety is my initial priority. I'll stand guard so you can get your children and yourselves outside and off-property, understood?"

"Yes, Mr. Cabernet," the father replied.

“Right,” Charlemagne said, hovering his finger over the trigger. “Go!”

The family got up from behind the table and ran into the foyer, causing two hovering objects, a white Japanese tea cup and matching teapot, to rise from a slim table in the corridor and be thrown at them. Charlemagne responded by opening fire and having a white beam shoot out of his gun and hit the carpet near the table, leaving a smoldering black stained hole that revealed the hardwood floor underneath. He ensured that the family had left before lowering the cannon with one hand and bringing down his thermal goggles to look ahead.

Charlemagne tried to find the ghost but couldn’t see any abnormal cold spots before him. He quickly turned off the goggles and then brought up the cannon again. Charlemagne began to make his way forward and over the dining table to get out of the room and head into the hall ahead. He came into the quiet corridor and found himself choosing between three ways: another door leading outside on the right, continuing down the corridor ahead, or entering the kitchen on the left. Charlemagne chose to continue forward, entering a living room.

The living room had a white carpet and beige walls with little furniture around. There was a desk in the corner, a brown couch in the middle looking to the TV and wall. On the right of the couch was a rocking chair, swinging back and forth with nobody physically atop of it. Charlemagne froze for a moment as he stared at the phenomenon. He brought the cannon down to switch on the thermal goggles and see before him where a light blue cold spot existed at the seat of the rocking chair.

Charlemagne readied the cannon, raising it up to aim at the chair only to have it pulled up, causing him to fall backwards onto the floor. An immense chill passed through him, seeping through his thermal jumpsuit as though someone had splashed him with water that didn't leave him wet and quickly dried. Charlemagne looked up at the ceiling with the heavy cannon resting against his torso. He pushed it to the side so he could get up before picking it up again. He looked around the room from where he stood with concentrated breathing. However, the cold spot was out of sight.

Noise came from the kitchen alongside the shattering of glass. Charlemagne made his way back, pausing just before the archway into the kitchen where he saw the refrigerator door open (as the refrigerator behind the wall immediately next to him). He slowly crept forward, brushing himself against the wall as he extended a hand from the cannon and brought it over the stainless steel surface of the refrigerator door. The door suddenly shut close. Charlemagne retreated his hand and jumped around the corner with the cannon ready to fire.

Charlemagne was rushed again as he felt the cold wind come against him, pushing him back. However, he still fired into the ceiling as he saw the blue spot above him on the ceiling. A white beam shot out from the cannon, firing up and causing wood to shred above him. Charlemagne came to lose grip of the beam as it was tossed to the side without causing any damage to the environment around until the last moments before he released his grip from the trigger. It was as though he had grabbed ahold of the entity and it resisted. The curtain in the living room above the TV was the sole casualty as it was sliced in half.

The cold spot rushed around in a frenzy as Charlemagne laid on the ground. It then disappeared out of sight again. Charlemagne knocked the cannon aside and then brushed off the dust from the ceiling from his jumpsuit. He then stood up and picked up the cannon again.

“Where’d you go?” Charlemagne grunted as he knelt down for a moment to wipe sweat from his forehead. “Where did you go, my dear?”

Charlemagne forced himself back onto both feet. His hands were sweaty and trembled at the handles of the cannon. He breathed steadily, but hard, and his forehead was wet again as he stepped into the kitchen and made his way deeper into the house. Charlemagne arrived at a junction between another corridor, leading to a single door or continuing to the end of the current corridor which branched into two rooms on either side. Charlemagne continued to the end and peaked into each of these bedrooms, both of which were empty. He then came to the end of the other corridor, which led into a master bedroom. It was empty as well.

“Bleeding hell,” Charlemagne cursed as he closed the door to the master bedroom. Where the bloody hell did it go? Don’t tell me it’s gone…”

Charlemagne returned to the kitchen before entering the foyer. He turned on the lights of the foyer and sitting room as it had now grown dark, and took from his belt a small device that looked like a plasma canister, but was entirely made of metal. He set it on the middle of a rug in the foyer. Charlemagne triggered the device on its timer, buying him time to come into the dining room and kneel down.

There, Charlemagne took the opportunity to wipe some more sweat from his forehead before readying the cannon. The device opened a hatch atop of itself, which exhausted some heat upwards. Charlemagne watched the redness through his goggles before he spotted the cold spot come down from the attic above and surround the trap. The heat gradually rose from the device and a mist of ectoplasm began to breeze away, dropping onto the edge of the rug like dew.

"Fascinating," Charlemagne noted as he watched.

The device began to overheat and plasma developed around where the cold spot was like veins to the entity. The phenomenon froze it place. Charlemagne stood up and fired the cannon at the creature, creating immediate resistance as Charlemagne dug his feet into the hardwood floor. The trap beneath the creature exploded, freeing the creature to pull away from the white beam and dragging Charlemagne forward.

Charlemagne lost his grip and took two steps forward but regained his ground as the being attempted to escape him. The creature began to pull the beam towards the wide window in the sitting room, but Charlemagne held his ground as he tried to pull it into the vacuum of the plasma beam. The resistance of the entity was strong. The cannon vibrated as it was attempted to take the being and Charlemagne's grip was weakening as he lost stamina.

"Come on…" Charlemagne grunted as he clenched his teeth.

Charlemagne came forward again without even taking a step as he was dragged a good inch towards the French window steps into the foyer from the dining room. He looked down at the step with fear. He then looked up and towards the being as he eyed the light fixture above the coffee table in the sitting room. Charlemagne then began to try and redirect the beam towards it.

The light fixture cracked and sent sparks flying below. Plasma enflamed the being again, causing it to freeze. Charlemagne then stood up onto the steps of the French window and stepped forward towards the creature until suddenly, in a bright light, all resistance as well as the beam cut off entirely. The cannon recoiled and Charlemagne felt the pleasure of his muscles resting as he fell forward on both knees in a pant. He held one hand on the handle of the cannon, which was still vibrating.

Quickly, Charlemagne twisted the cap and removed the plasma container and set it aside where he saw a dark yellow haze instead of the initial green plasma. He then got onto one knee and proceeded to dry his forehead with his sleeve.

Charlemagne eventually stood up, grabbed the container by the top and his cannon with the other hand, and left the house. The crisp late summer, early night air was refreshing to him as he faced the family and a crowd of curious neighbors at the base of the driveway.

"It's over," Charlemagne announced, joining the crowd with the canister.

"What is that?" a man asked.

"Was there really a ghost?" a woman questioned.

"I wouldn't jump to the conclusion that it was a 'ghost,' but whatever it was, it's entrapped in here now."

"Oh, thank God it's over," the mother replied to Charlemagne, clasping both hands together.

"Thank you, really," the father added.

"Are you sure you're not being scammed here?" a man asked.

"Don't be silly," a woman replied.

"Then again… it is Charlemagne," another woman added.

"If you'd please," Charlemagne said to the parents. "I have some questions I'd like to ask you inside the house."

"Certainly," the mother replied. "Come on, kids."

Charlemagne put the cannon into the back of the truck and stored the ghost into the appropriate container as the neighbors dispersed. He then walked behind the parents and their children to their home.

"Oh my God," the mother reacted as she saw the mess at the rug.

The mother let go of her children's hands and rushed in further to see the mess around.

"Oh my God!" she shouted. "What is this mess?!"

"Rest assured, ma'am, that I tried to limit as much damage as I could," Charlemagne said. "Be careful, however, ma'am! Do not touch that substance on the rug! It's a biohazard."

The mother had fallen to her knees and sat at the rug. She moved her hand away from the ectoplasm as she proceeded to cry.

"Why us?" she muttered.

"Kids, why don't you go to your rooms," the father said, seeing them off before crouching down to see to his wife.

"If I could interrupt," Charlemagne sheepishly said. "I have a few questions to finish my investigation here."

"Sure," the father replied, annoyed. "What is it?"

"Firstly, if I could inquire into what occurred prior to my arrival, which would be the best place to begin," Charlemagne responded, taking out a notebook and pen.

"What do you want me to say?" the father said. "I suppose it began when we were sitting down for dinner and I came into the kitchen to refresh my drink. I noticed that the oven was still on and that the oven door was open. I tried to close it, but it just opened again. Then I slammed it closed, and my scotch threw itself to the other side of the room. My wife wondered what had happened and came in. She thought I was doing all that, but then when she came into the kitchen, she got pushed back onto the ground. Then a bunch of shoes by her at the side door were thrown at me. My wife thought to call the police, but I stopped her out of fear that they'd think we were pranking them or crazy. Then my wife remembered that she got an email from your company about paranormal disturbances and to call you if one ever occurred… so we did that."

"I see," Charlemagne replied. "Tell me, have you had any recently deceased livestock or domestic animals in the two or three years?"

"What? No."

"Any relatives?"

"No. No death."

"Understood."

"Is… is this going to cost anything? I mean, I don't know if we can cover the damages as well as paying you…"

"Don't you worry about that," Charlemagne replied, producing a business card. "I do not charge for these visits – for the way I see it, you did me more of a favor in notifying about this for my research. In fact, if you contact the number on this card, I'll ensure that a contractor comes to assess these damages and write you a cheque of compensation for these damages."

"Really?" the father questioned. "Why?"

Both the mother and father looked up to him.

"I already told you," Charlemagne remarked with a smirk. "You've done me an immense favor by leading me here to capture this 'spirit' so I am in debt to you."

"Thank you," the father said, squeezing the hand of his wife. "Thank you!"

The couple's sorrow turned into smiles as they hugged each other.

"Do you have any more questions for us?"

"Not at the moment," Charlemagne replied. "I'll contact you should that change. I'll leave you two at the moment to rest, but if I may, could I take your rug with me for the sample."

"Sure, sure," the father remarked, standing up with his wife.

The couple moved to the couch in the sitting room while Charlemagne rolled up the rug. He then picked it up and said goodbye to the couple before leaving. Charlemagne put the rug in the back of the pickup truck, closed the canopy and then came to the driver's seat.

The weather turned to rain as Charlemagne drove back to the mansion. He parked the truck in the garage and went around to retrieve the capsule containing the entity. He then went to the elevator and went upstairs to the kitchen. Charlemagne came to his lab and closed the door behind him. He set the entrapped entity onto the table in the middle and sat at his stool. He produced from a drawer a voice recorder and set it on the table.

Charlemagne then stood up and went to go fill his kettle with some water before bringing it to sit on a hot plate. He removed half of his jumpsuit so that his undershirt was exposed. He also opened the door to the balcony to let fresh air in. Charlemagne then brought his notebook and set it on the table. He began to stare at the yellow haze in the capsule until his eyes showed that he was lost and the entity stared back at him.

The whistling of the kettle eventually broke Charlemagne's attention, causing him to stand up and pour himself a cup of tea. He then sat down again and pressed record on the voice recorder.

"On September 7th, 2017, at approximately 2030 hours, I was notified by mobile alert of a disturbance at 1290 Wilbur Avenue."

Charlemagne then went into detail about the event until he finished and paused for a moment.

"The field test of the plasma beam cannon proved successful. The plasma storage capsule successfully held the entity and continues to hold the entity. However, at the present in my workshop, I have no mechanism capable of being able to perform tests on the being. The trap I made performed well but short-circuited too slowly and the electrocution it procured onto the entity was minor and didn't stun the entity as much as I had hoped."

Charlemagne paused for another moment.

"In regard to the attraction of these entities to sources of heat, I have also been able to hypothesize the 'cold' nature of these creatures but have not been able to rationalize the production of ectoplasm. The color of this entity has also posed some curiosity that I have not been able to rationalize either.

I am sure that the nature of this entity, if it could be called a 'spirit,' is human. The behavior of the entity around the house was specifically human, even if it was savage behavior. However, like the supposed 'dog' perhaps this behavior is not implicit and instead explicit to the conditions. On the other hand, one could explain the spirit to belong to an Amerindian buried underneath the suburbs of Allabrese. Both hypotheses are likely and not necessarily mutually exclusive.

In order to collect more data and answer some of these questions, I will need to expand the resources available to me, such as contacting… friends, if I can even consider any to be left in the scientific community… Regardless, the path forward would be to extend our knowledge on the subject of these entities. End of report."

Act 3, Scene 3

Charlemagne sat in his office at Cabernet Industries Head Office. It was a room similar in size to his study in the manor, but with a distinct change in architecture. His office was simple with grey painted walls. Behind his desk was a large window with blinds pulled back on either side. It looked out to downtown Allabrese and the grey clouds of the mid-autumn day. The rest of the office had little decoration. On the right from the desk, against the wall were bookcases with few books. Between the bookcases was a glass table pressed against the wall with various items atop. Behind this table, on the wall, was a painting.

In front of Charlemagne's desk were two armchairs where two men in suits sat across from Charlemagne. Behind the couches was a carpet and at the opposite side of the room was a fireplace with a couch in front of it. To the right of the couch was a glass wall and glass door going into the corridor outside the office. Above the carpet in the middle room was a chandelier. One of the men across from Charlemagne was a man named Ian Frank, Charlemagne's personal attorney and chief legal counsel for Cabernet Industries. Next to this man was Richard Huxley. Mr. Frank was slightly younger than Charlemagne, but older than Huxley. He had black hair that was thinning at a widow's peak. He wore a blue suit with a black tie and was of a medium build.

"The Medici's attorneys wish to meet once more later this week to discuss the usual topic of dropping charges against their Duce," Ian Frank informed Charlemagne.

"To hell with them," Charlemagne responded. "I won't have any more of these meetings with them. If Giovanni wishes to speak to me, I will have a private word with him, but until then, our correspondences will be formal and brief until the court date."

"Are you sure about that, Charles?" Huxley questioned. "The Medici clan is adamant on having these charges against Giovanni dropped."

"I won't be intimidated by their medieval techniques," Charlemagne replied, taking off his glasses to look to him and Mr. Frank. "I expect some decency from the so-called head of the Medici family. For all the sins that Nero Medici had committed, at least the tyrant had courage to meet his foes face-to-face. I wouldn't even have charges dropped on my own brother, and they think I'll lower charges on this thug?"

A loud noise overwhelmed the room met with the vibration of the building and push of a blast. Charlemagne lowered his head before spinning around in his seat. He turned to face outside, looking towards the library across from the head office where either smoke or steam was dissipating from the Curtia Dawson Public Library – a Gothic structure of neo-baroque style. It had a rusted copper domed top and overlooked the central park. It was a medium-sized building. Various members of the public were leaving the building at a fast pace.

Charlemagne simply looked with curiosity and seriousness. His phone then vibrated behind him on his desk. The sounds of fire engine sirens could be heard on approach. Charlemagne turned around and picked up his phone. He looked at the alert and saw that it was an incoming automatic SMS notification detailing a dispatch of a paranormal disturbance at the public library.

"Good Lord," Charlemagne reacted, putting his phone away. "Sorry, but I must leave now."

Charlemagne turned around from his desk and moved to exit his office. He then passed his receptionist and went to the elevators, calling for an elevator. When the elevator arrived, he entered and selected to go downstairs to the parking garage. Once there, he walked over to where the grey pickup truck was parked. He opened the canopy in the back and pulled out a briefcase with his uniform in it. He then started to get changed in the garage, putting his clothing away inside and then entering the truck to start the engine.

The pickup truck quickly pulled out and exited the garage. It made a short trip from behind the office and around to the front entrance of the library where two fire engines had arrived with firefighters on the scene. Charlemagne stopped his vehicle nearby and got out. He then went around to collect his gear before looking out to the various firefighters. He recognized one of them and immediately set forward to talk to him. He was an older man about 5'10" in height with short white hair, about a decade younger than Charlemagne and with a moustache.

"Chief Rowan," Charlemagne greeted.

"What the hell do you think you're doing here, Charles?" Rowan complained. "Who called for you?"

"I'm not sure, but I was called to attend here," Charlemagne replied. "What's happened?"

"The fire panel is clear, but there's some sort of system trouble. All this steam tells me that it's some sort of issue with the boiler – possibly blown. I have boys from Engine Ten going down to the sublevel to report back. We might need to cut water flow to the library, which'll mean that it'll have to be shut down."

"Do you permit me to enter the scene?"

"Not a chance, Charles," Rowan replied. "Honestly, you may as well just leave. There's no ghost for you here. Whoever called you must have been mistaken or wanted to see a show. I'm sorry."

Some static began to come through the fire chief's radio.

"Engine Nine, we're definitely dealing with a blown boiler…"

Static picked up again.

"Say again?" Chief Rowan replied.

All but static came through.

"There's something going on here," the radio replied before static followed.

The radio transmitted screams coming from the firefighters followed by a high-pitched screech. The radio then produced static and then went dead.

"Engine Nine, come in?" Chief Rowan demanded.

No reply came through. The chief then looked at Charlemagne.

"I'm sure it was nothing," the chief replied, putting on his helmet and picking up a spare. "Come on, if it'll get you off my back, come with me. Here, you'll have to wear this."

Charlemagne took the fire helmet and placed it on. He then followed the fire chief around the fire engine and up the steps towards the library entrance. They were joined by another two firefighters.

The main entrance of the library was a large and open room with staircases on either side going up to the second floor. Immediately in front, between the staircases was a checkout desk, and on either side of the stairs were the spaces where shelves containing thousands of books were. The room was filled and thick with steam. It was warm.

Charlemagne produced a device from his belt, which was small and handheld. It was about the size of an old cellphone and displayed a screen with numbers and a semicircular meter. At the present, the device was displaying low numbers and sticking the left side of the meter. Charlemagne followed the fire chief towards the checkout desk and behind it to enter a staff only zone. They went through the office space in the back and towards a door that led to a staircase downstairs. The steam was thicker here and it was harder to see. The aesthetics transitioned from regal and wooden to simple and concrete.

Once Charlemagne had arrived at the basement, his device began to show higher numbers and the meter swung to the right. The ground was flooded with water about one-two inches high.

"I'm picking up normal oxygen levels down here," a firefighter remarked, reaching a set of doors.

Charlemagne jerked his head to a doorway to the side as he noticed a breeze rush by, hitting him with a light zephyr that contrasted with the steamy surroundings. The device in his hand also peaked its readings.

"Did anyone else feel that?" Charlemagne asked the firefighters in front.

"Feel what?" Chief Rowan replied in dull tone, turning around to look at Charlemagne.

"A light wind from the parallel corridor," Charlemagne explained. "I picked up a burst of electromagnetic energy when it passed. A cold wind is typically a sign of a spirit passing by."

The other firefighters looked at each other as the fire chief shook his head. He then turned around and continued forward. They came into a dark room where each of them took out flashlights to bring some light. The room was purely for storage with boxes stacked around. They continued into the next corridor with their flashlights and entered another room where two firefighters could be seen with their backs against the wall. Each of them were dazed, but conscious. They looked up and over to their colleagues who rushed towards them.

"Macleod, are you alright?" Rowan questioned to one, crouching down to check on him. "What happened?"

“I- I don’t know,” Macleod replied. “What’s going on?”

“You’re cold, son,” Rowan remarked, taking his hand from the firefighter’s forehead. “You’re also looking pale. Do you remember anything?”

“No…” Macleod replied.

“Chief, Ferdinandsen isn’t looking too good either. I can’t even get a response from him,” the other firefighter explained.

“I’m shutting the water off – hopefully that should stop all this steam,” the third firefighter said, turning a valve.

“Good,” Chief Rowan replied, looking back at Macleod. “Come on, let’s get you out of here.”

The other firefighters helped Ferdinandsen onto his feet. He was unable to keep his feet on the ground, but

“Charles, don’t just stand there,” Rowan complained. “Show some use and help me out.”

Charlemagne put his device away and helped Rowan. Each of them took a shoulder and helped the firefighter onto his feet. He was weak and unable to stand on his own, so they helped him out from the basement and upstairs.

The two firefighters were brought out of the library and down the steps towards the ambulances that had arrived to assist. The paramedics hurried over with their stretchers, lowering them so that each firefighter could take a seat. The chief and other firefighters then started to help unload some equipment from them.

Charlemagne stuck nearby, looking at the paramedics as they assessed each of the firefighters. He could see for himself that they had pale skin and from what he could read from the thermometers, low temperatures. They were also shivering and had an elevated breathing rate, but not dramatically. Charlemagne turned his attention from the patients to the pair of police cars that had just arrived. He immediately frowned as he saw Chief Phillips exit.

"What seems to be the problem here?" Phillips questioned, passing by Charlemagne and ignoring him.

"From what we've gathered so far," Chief Rowan replied, "a blown boiler. We've turned off the water and that should stop any further structural damage."

"And what's he doing here?" Phillips questioned, looking at Charlemagne.

"He was called to attend because of supposed paranormal activity," Rowan explained.

"What's so paranormal about a boiler blowing up?" Phillips asked.

"Well, we are unsure of the cause of the boiler blowing up, but two of my men who were sent to investigate went silent on us and when we went to check, I found them both with mild hypothermia," Rowan said to him.

"So, they got a little cold, and?"

"It was about thirty degrees Celsius below the library," Rowan further explained. "I have no idea how both of them could have developed mild hypothermia."

"And I did notice a high-reading of EMF energy as well," Charlemagne added, interrupting. "I insist that I must return to investigate the spirit wandering the library."

"Not a chance, Charles," Phillips replied. "Not a chance."

"With all due respect," Rowan responded. "I'm afraid that you don't get to make that call. I'm in charge here, and I believe there is no harm in sending Charlemagne in to investigate further. I've read the papers – I'm familiar with his 'expertise' in the matter, and after seeing what I saw… I think I might just trust him."

Charlemagne looked at the fire chief and then over to the police chief. Chief Phillips cheeks had grown red. He held a frown and then turned around to leave. Chief Rowan then looked to Charlemagne who was standing there.

"Well, what are you waiting for?" Rowan questioned. "I'm going to maintain my team's presence here until you give us the clear. Here."

Rowan handed Charlemagne a radio.

"Give us a call when you can if you need immediate help or if all is clear," Rowan explained.

"Certainly," Charlemagne replied, nodding.

Charlemagne rushed back to the pickup truck to pull a reinforced case with his beam cannon inside. He took it out, held it in his hands and then went over to the front steps of the library. He turned around to look at the various firefighters and two policemen who were looking at him. He then turned back forward to go up the steps and into the library again as he looked at the title of the library, Curtia Dawson Memorial Library, etched into the top above the doorway.

The inside of the library was dark. He took out his EMF reader and saw there to be a mild level of electromagnetic energy in the area. He then put it away and lowered his thermal goggles as he made his way left into a large open room with various tables spread around. At the back of the room, near some tall windows was a long desk with various computers in a row. Behind this common room were three tall rows of bookshelves, labeled 'Youth Books.'

The power was out and the area was not dark, but the only source of light came out of the windows, which was minimal on this grey day. Charlemagne stepped forward to the center of the room and then immediately turned towards the bookshelves as he spotted a cold blur pass behind the bookshelf in front of him.

He readied his weapon but could not see the spirit again. The being had caused some books to fly off the shelf and land on the ground. Charlemagne lowered his weapon and continued to look around the room.

Suddenly, the cold spot, which was much larger than previous spirits, such as the one seen at Wilbur, passed by again, causing the furthest bookshelf to tip over from its base, hitting the one in the middle, which then hit the one closer to Charlemagne. Charlemagne looked at the bookshelf tipping over and then immediately started to rush towards the side of the room, pushing chairs away from his path as it started to come down. He reached the side of the room and brought his back against it as the shelf fell upon the tables and chairs, smashing some of them in its wake.

A large cloud of dust lifted upwards before dissipating into the ceiling. Charlemagne struggled to get out of the east wing of the ground floor and came to the foyer. He crossed into the west wing and took out a new device on his belt. He turned off his thermal goggles to look at the device.

The device was vertical and had a pull out display on the side with a grid-like pattern. It was held by a handle, similar to one found on a nail gun, but the top had been replaced with squared top. It was dark grey in color. Charlemagne looked at the black screen. He then began to walk into the west wing, which was simply rows upon rows of bookshelves.

Charlemagne walked along and kept his eyes on the scanner. He made a thorough patrol through the perimeter of the west wing before coming back to the foyer. There were no sightings of the ghost. However, various books could be seen among the aisles as if they had been pulled out from the bookshelves and left on the ground. After Charlemagne had finished in the west wing, he began to go up the closest staircase to the second floor where he could start to see a signature towards the right of him. Charlemagne looked over with his naked eye to the railings where there was nothing. He then turned on his goggles, switching to a new ultraviolet setting provided to him by Cabernet Laboratories to see in front of him a will-o-wisp of almost lavender-like blue strands of light dancing in front of him. Charlemagne stared at the creature. It then passed him and spun around, flying around the central foyer of the library.

The wisp flew around, slowly and majestically as Charlemagne walked towards the center of the railings. The spirit then came down so that it was right in front of him. Charlemagne could feel the coldness around him. Charlemagne's breath was visible in a cloud of vapor. The ghost then floated off and disappeared behind him.

Charlemagne attempted to follow the creature, entering a large ballroom behind him, atop of the offices behind the reception desk. The room was circular with a combination of desks against the walls as well as old paintings and portraits against the walls. There were also tall windows and a large chandelier dangling from the middle of the ceiling. The floor was polished wood. He entered the room and saw the wisp moving around. Charlemagne took a device out from his belt and prepared it. He then tossed it to the middle, letting it open and exhaust heat upwards.

The wisp went towards the heat source where ectoplasm began to develop in a cloud that harmlessly drifted away from both the creature and Charlemagne. Charlemagne readied the beam cannon to take aim at the creature, but as he did so, he noticed a spherical ball of ectoplasm developing and spinning in a circle. The tiny ball grew bigger and bigger until it was about the size of a watermelon. Charlemagne had lowered his cannon to witness this when suddenly, the ball of ectoplasm had shot at him.

Charlemagne quickly moved to get out of the way of the projectile, but the ball had hit him in the right arm regardless, covering the left sleeve of his jumpsuit in the goo. The impact of the projectile caused him to flex his arm to absorb the shock and regardless, it caused his arm to recoil backwards slightly. Charlemagne tried to shake the substance as he felt it vibrating. He then quickly turned his attention back to the spirit as it began to fire another one towards him.

This time, Charlemagne jumped out of the way before quickly standing up as the trap was about to spring. Charlemagne turned to face the creature as the trap induced an electrical shock. He fired his cannon and caught the creature within the gravitational pull of the plasma beam shot at it. Immediately, he felt resistance that pulled back. Charlemagne held on until the trap exploded and the shocks ended.

The creature was free and pulled against Charlemagne, dragging him forward as the creature approached the surrounding wall. The creature then broke free. Charlemagne's beam of plasma shot against the wall, slashing a portrait in half and singeing the walls with a straight line that broke into a tall window. Charlemagne immediately removed his hands from the trigger and traced the spirit with his eyes as it spun around the ceiling. It had made about three laps around the large ceiling within seconds when Charlemagne noticed it had been forming another ball of ectoplasm.

Charlemagne looked at the creature with hazardous eyes, seeing the ball get bigger and bigger the more laps the creature created. Once the ball of ectoplasm was about the size of a cantaloupe, Charlemagne had no other option but to open fire. A beam of plasma shot at the ceiling, ripping through. The creature broke its cyclic pattern and shot the ball of ectoplasm towards Charlemagne. It fell upon him like a coconut from the sky, causing him to lower his weapon and quickly run out of its path.

The ectoplasm dropped down and made a splash upon impact. The creature then threw more balls towards him as it danced around and they formed. Charlemagne rushed to the other side of the room and then fired the beam cannon towards it. The spirit disappeared.

Charlemagne tensed his finger around the trigger of the cannon. He looked around, waiting for the spirit to re-emerge and scanning every direction with anticipation. He saw the spirit emerge from the east, causing him to flinch at its sudden appearance, but quickly turn and cover his head.

The spirit rushed into him, soaking his back and the fibers of his thermal jumpsuit. He could feel the coldness upon him despite his personal protection but was able to stand up and look as it returned to the ceiling to dance around. Charlemagne eyed the spirit in the chandelier and frowned at it. It began to toss ectoplasm towards him.

Charlemagne rushed out of the way and to the other side of the ballroom, away from the entrance. He took out his radio and started to run back, dodging the pool of the ectoplasm on the ground. He then took cover by the door hinge and brought the radio to his mouth.

“This is Charlemagne,” Charlemagne announced, “I need you to restore power to the library.”

There was a moment of silence as Charlemagne looked around the side. The spirit had disappeared. He dropped a surprised look and re-entered the ballroom with hesitant steps. He looked at every single side with anticipation.

“Copy that, Charlie,” a voice responded from the radio.

Charlemagne briefly looked at the radio and then put it back on his belt. Suddenly, the spirit made its appearance again from the northside. Charlemagne saw it charge towards him. Instead of moving out of the way, he charged his cannon at it. The spirit immediately detracted from its path to move up, pulling Charlemagne up with it and causing him to let go.

The spirit then flew up as Charlemagne noticed lights turn on from the rest of the library. He took the chance to rush to the entrance into the ballroom where he saw the light switch for the room. Charlemagne went over, turned it on and brightened the room through the chandelier. The spirit immediately began to dance around the lightbulbs, but with the warmth of the incandescent light bulbs, the spirit began to produce balls of ectoplasm. Charlemagne immediately fired his cannon into the light, causing light bulbs to burst open and sparks to fly. He drew the beam right into the stem of the chandelier, causing it to drop down slightly with its wiring and further sparks to fly about. The spirit was paralyzed with all of the electrical activity, letting Charlemagne pull at it.

The spirit was still able to resist. Charlemagne stepped forward. He drew the beam into the wiring. Flashes filled the room, causing Charlemagne to close his eyes. The beam cannon vibrated, but Charlemagne did not let go. He held his ground and could hear the crash of the chandelier collapsing onto the floor. A cloud of dust and debris flew past him, cutting at his face. Charlemagne opened his eyes briefly and then it was over.

The beam cannon had shut off and recoiled, triggering Charlemagne to immediately empty it of the canister. He took it out and held it in his hands. He then turned off his goggles and kept the beam cannon on the ground as he looked at the bluish haze inside. Charlemagne admired the sight before noticing that ectoplasm was seeping through the top of the canister.

Charlemagne held the canister at a different angle and set it on the floor. He then took out his cellphone and dialed. He brought the phone to his ear.

"This is Charlemagne – alert Dr. Lambert that I'm coming in with a live specimen. Have her prepare the chamber."

Charlemagne then hung up and put his phone away. He grabbed the radio and brought it to his mouth.

"This is Charlie," Charlemagne announced. "The structure is clear."

Charlemagne then put the radio away and grabbed his cannon. He picked it up and then grabbed the canister. Charlemagne then began to make his exit at a fast pace with both in hand.

Act 3, Scene 4

Charlemagne pulled in to the front of Cabernet Laboratories main building and got out of the pick-up truck to rush to the rear of the car. Two scientists as well as security were there waiting for him. The security officers employed by Cabernet Industries wore brown collared shirts tucked into brown cargo pants. They also wore ties underneath the black ballistic vests over their shirts as well as paramilitary belts with handcuffs. The standard for each officer was to wear brown boots in addition to this getup. Charlemagne pulled the container and grabbed it by the top of the handle. He then came through the main entrance sliding doors where the others awaited him.

"Mr. Cabernet," a man said.

Charlemagne ignored and passed by them. He made his pass by the receptionist desk, fountain and artwork of images taken from microscopes.

"Are they ready?" Charlemagne yelled.

"Ready for you in the sublevel," a receptionist replied.

"Good."

Charlemagne made his way down the main hallway where a maintenance elevator was being held for him. He entered with several people before the doors closed and they went down. The doors then opened again for the convoy of people to exit and enter the sub-basement corridor. Charlemagne grasped his hand tightly around the handle of the crate and hastened his pace. The group came to a pair of sliding doors that entered a vestibule, which then led into a larger room. Each door was locked and required a proxy keycard to enter. Charlemagne had security tapping him through.

Inside the larger laboratory was a large tube in the middle with a reinforced base and appendix where a plasma canister could be inserted. The machine was surrounded by desks and computers on a platform as well as a protected room with reinforced glass and additional computers.

Charlemagne stepped down and settled the crate near the appendix.

"Everybody back," the voice of a woman shouted.

Charlemagne opened the crate, which was seeping and oozing with ectoplasm. He carefully picked up the capsule and brought it to the machine to insert. He then turned the lid before giving a thumbs up to those in the protective room. The room filled with a red light and the sound of an alarm going off. Charlemagne went up the steps of a platform and went to join the rest of the staff inside the protective room.

There, the lights turned green and a swooshing sound was heard. Lights in the room flickered as the machine purred and the contents of the vat were replaced with physically nothing, but in reality the captured entity entrapped by the electromagnetic chamber. Plasma could be seen like lightning every so often as the vat had become virtually a thundercloud without the cloud.

"It's secured," a man said at a computer.

The rest of the team began to clap and some even patted Charlemagne on the back. Charlemagne took a deep breath as he relaxed.

"Well done," the voice of a woman in a Londoner accent said.

Charlemagne turned around and looked at the woman. She was younger than Charlemagne, but not by much. She was middle-aged, in her fifties, but showed limited signs of aging. Her hair was still the same natural light blonde it had always been, and she was as elegant as ever. She wore a lab coat over her designer sweater and wore a black skirt with dark brown leggings.

"Dr. Lambert..." Charlemagne replied.

"Dr. Lambert?" she replied

"Judith," Charlemagne corrected himself.

"I had all of this as soon as I got the word from you," Dr. Lambert said. "I just everything is to your specifications."

"It is. Thank you."

Dr. Lambert looked at Charlemagne with pity as she held her tablet to the side of her torso. She stepped forward to Charlemagne and tilted her head.

"What color was this one in the plasma capsule?" Judith questioned, tapping into her tablet.

"Blue," Charlemagne replied, walking out of the control room with Dr. Lambert. "Also, there's plenty of ectoplasm for your team to analyze and determine an ethnic origin to this creature."

"Excellent," Dr. Lambert remarked as the two walked. "You know, Charlemagne, all of us appreciate the work you're doing outside in the field. Especially me."

"It's no problem. Really. This one was a voracious one, I must say."

The two paused from their walk as they stood in front of the vat. Charlemagne looked inside and through the tinted glass with both hands behind his back, admiring the sight with a serious face. He then turned to Dr. Lambert as she tilted her head and looked at Charlemagne with focused eyes.

"Is something wrong, Charles?" Judith asked.

"No," Charlemagne denied. "Why?"

"It's just... I was taken back by how you addressed me as 'Dr. Lambert' or how you never contacted me in person when it came to preparing this room."

Charlemagne looked to the side and away from both the vat and Dr. Lambert. He didn't respond for a moment.

"Charles?"

"My apologies, of course. You are correct. Please accept my apology."

"Yes," Dr. Lambert replied. "However, I must ask where you've been all this time. I haven't seen you in at least a year, and there was talk of you selling Cabernet Industries during the start of the year…"

"Nevermind that," Charlemagne replied. "What's important is that it's over and I've moved on."

"Right…" Judith said. "Well, don't you forget, Charles, that no matter where you are, you can always rely on me. We've known each other for decades… a friendship like that can never deteriorate."

Dr. Lambert took Charlemagne's cold hands, causing him to quickly retract them.

"I appreciate your support, my dear," Charlemagne replied.

"Don't forget it," Dr. Lambert smiled. "You're a brilliant mind, Charlemagne."

"Of course," Charlemagne affirmed. "Right, well, I'll leave you to get back to it. The sooner we can unravel the origin of these mysterious spiritual disturbances, the better."

"I wholeheartedly agree, Charles. We're still not sure as to what these spirits are, but we are, but the frequency of these spirits consisting of Amerindian DNA has more or less told us that these are remnants of the deceased. That begs the question of what is causing them to arise as they are, or why this is happening now and here of all times and places."

"Something is disturbing the natural balance," Charlemagne said.

Charlemagne smiled to Judith as he finished his sentence.

"Regardless of where they come from, they need to recognize that they are out of their underworld. In these lands, we are the rulers and we do not tolerate their behavior."

"Of course, Judy," Charlemagne assured her.

Charlemagne looked back into the vat as he crossed his arms.

"You can't let them keep me here," a voice whispered in Charlemagne's ear.

Charlemagne's skin grew pale and his eyes widened. His ear twitched as he froze before looking to Dr. Lambert who was typing in her tablet as though she heard nothing.

"Judith," Charlemagne said.

"Yes, Charles," she replied.

"I'm- I'm afraid I must be going now. I must-"

"Is everything alright?"

"No – yes! Everything is fine. I just- I need to get some sleep, I believe. I've had a terribly long day. I should be going home now to have a nap."

"Of course, Charles," Dr. Lambert peacefully said. "The ghost isn't going anywhere and it's nearly four o'clock anyhow. I'll stick around for another hour or so, but then I'll have to leave too."

The two walked away from the vat and came to the exit. Dr. Lambert tapped her identification card before the two started to walk out.

"You'll make me have to save the bottle of champagne I had for this moment – perhaps to have another day to celebrate."

"Champagne?" Charlemagne questioned. "Why? There was nothing to celebrate here. We are only at the beginning of an enduring battle."

"If you say so, old friend," Dr. Lambert smiled.

Act 4, Scene 1

Five minutes were left until the bell as Tristan leaned back in his seat, waiting for his English class to end. He looked at his notes in his binder and over to the careless teacher who sat at her desk, marking essays while the other students chattered quietly.

Tristan lowered his head and took his phone out of his pocket, raising his head over to Diana at the front of the class with her friend, Moira Macmillan. He looked at Moira with a mild frown before looking back at Diana. He continued to look at them, causing his cheeks to redden.

"Whatever," Tristan whispered to himself, unlocking his phone to play a game before looking forward to Vivian Huxley.

Tristan caught gaze of her light brown hair and blonde highlights. He tried to eavesdrop on the conversation she was having with Maia Grayson (her best friend) next to her. He then looked over to Diana before looking back at Vivian.

"What are you going to do for Halloween?" Maia asked Vivian.

"I don't know," she replied. "I haven't thought much about the dance. Nobody's asked me… at least, nobody that I like."

Tristan dropped his frown and raised his eyes. He picked up his backpack and found a breath mint before putting it away. He then stood up and went over to the empty seat next to Vivian.

"Oh my God, turn around," Maia said to Vivian in a low voice and bright smile.

Vivian turned around with an equally bright smile as she saw Tristan. Tristan grinned at them as he sat in the desk next to hers.

"Hey, Tristie," Vivian flirtatiously greeted, turning to face him.

"Hey, Vivi," Tristan replied.

Diana immediately ears twitched as she heard the obnoxious giggling of Vivian. She dropped her smile and turned to face her, feeling her stomach kick as she saw Tristan with Vivian. She straightened in her desk and felt a frown come against her. Moira looked at Diana and rolled her eyes.

"Diana," Moira said.

"Sorry, what?" Diana questioned, turning her attention back to her best friend.

"You're unbelievable," Moira replied. "Do I have to ask again? Are you coming or not? Just tell me."

Diana looked at Moira to answer. Tristan continued to flirt with Vivian in the meantime.

"So, what are you up to?" Tristan asked.

"Oh… you know, nothing," Vivian replied. "What about you?"

"Isn't obvious?" Tristan said. "I'm talking to the- Sorry, I mean. I'm talking to a sweet girl like you, of course."

Diana growled at this and turned away from him. She tried to focus at the board in front of her with a blank face.

"Diana!" Moira scolded.

"Huh?" Diana replied. "What?"

"Are you coming or not!"

"Oh," Diana replied. "Yeah, of course. I'm not doing anything else *nor* do I have anybody else to hang out with."

Moira glared at her momentarily before they managed to keep talking. Diana managed to ignore Tristan despite the wide frown she continued to hold.

"So," Tristan said, "who has the honor of taking you to the Halloween dance this Tuesday?"

"Oh, I don't know. Nobody as of yet," Vivian replied. "Do you have any idea who might be able to handle me?"

Tristan laughed.

“I think I might,” Tristan said.

Diana turned her gaze to leer at Tristan as she heard his words. Her fists were clenched in the pockets of her red zip hoodie. The bell started to ring before the P.A. sounded with afterschool announcements. Once they were finished, the class was dismissed for the day.

The class stood from their seats to pack up and leave while Tristan went back to his desk and got his things. Moira left Diana behind as she put her things away. Maia and Vivian left behind her, and the rest of the seven other students left behind them. Tristan and Diana were the only ones left.

Tristan began to make his way out when Diana quickly rushed over to him and gently pushed him against the door frame.

“What the hell are you doing?” Tristan questioned as Diana pressed against his chest with a hand.

“What the hell am I doing?” Diana refracted. “What the hell are *you* doing?”

Tristan’s eyes widened as he looked at Diana. Diana could feel Tristan’s heart beating fast, causing her to let go for him to straighten up.

“What are you talking about?” Tristan questioned, giving a calm smile as he looked at her.

“I mean coming over from your desk to sit near me and annoy me,” Diana responded.

“Annoy you?” Tristan questioned and laughed. “Am I not allowed to talk to people in class?” he asked, stepping forward so that Diana was now against the opposite side of the door frame.

“No,” Diana replied.

“No, I’m not?”

"No, I mean-" Diana grunted. "I meant that you're not allowed to annoy me."

"And how does talking to Vivian annoy you?" Tristan remarked.

"That's a loaded question! You assume that it was you talking to Vivian that annoyed me. It was you talking in general!"

"Bug off!" Tristan remarked. "You're just being petty and jealous. You're not my girlfriend, Diana."

Diana laughed at him.

"No, luckily I'm not," she replied.

"Yeah, I knew the rumors about you and Moira being secret lovers was true then," Tristan said.

"What did you just say?" Diana questioned with an angry tone as she hit Tristan on the shoulder. "You're unbelievable – just because I'm not attracted to you, you make the assumption that I'm a dike? That Moira, somebody who's never done *anything* to you, is my 'secret lover?' She's my friend. And do you know why she's my friend? She's my friend because she is genuine with me. She doesn't pretend to be somebody she isn't at home or at school with me. She doesn't annoy me or make me frustrated. You do that, because you're not my friend, Tristan. So leave me alone and just don't talk to me."

Diana stepped to the side and walked away with a serious face. Tristan continued to stand where he was with shock.

"Crap," Tristan muttered to himself. "Diana," he shouted, entering the hallway only to see that she was gone

Diana came to her locker near the cafeteria and met with Moira nearby. She took a deep breath and fixed her hair into a ponytail. She then stood up tall and proud as she looked at Moira packing her homework into her backpack.

"What's up?" Moira asked as Diana took another deep breath.

"Oh, nothing really," Diana remarked. "I just cannot stand how Tristan can be sometimes. Do you know what he said – what he did?"

Diana paused for a moment before sighing and closing her eyes.

"Sorry, I was just referring to the way he was behaving in English before the bell just to spite me."

"Spite you?" Moira questioned. "How?"

"Didn't you notice? Him flirting with Vivian – that's how."

"And you think he did that to annoy you?"

"Duh," Diana replied. "He thinks that I like him. I just talked to him and he told me! The nerves of him too…"

"Okay then," Moira remarked. "Is that all? Are you done with this daily rant about Tristan or can I change the subject?"

Diana tilted her head slightly as she looked at Moira with a puzzling look.

"Daily? I do not talk about him daily," Diana remarked.

"Whatever you say," Moira said, closing her locker. "Let's go."

Act 4, Scene 2

Tristan stepped out of school and searched around for Diana along the front entrance, still feeling upset and regretful about what he did and said. Instead, he saw Charlemagne near the parking lot in front of the gym in the pickup truck. The engine was running and Charlemagne was inside the car. Tristan walked over and entered the car. Charlemagne noticed the sunken look on his face before looking around the front entrance for Diana. He then looked back at Tristan.

"Afternoon," Charlemagne greeted with a stern tone. "Is everything alright?"

"Yeah, I'm fine," Tristan responded. "What's with picking us up in this piece of crap?"

"Oh, it's a long story, but where's Diana?"

"Who knows," Tristan remarked, crossing his arms as he looked out the window. "Probably with her *friend* or something."

Charlemagne's phone vibrated. He picked it up and read the message on the screen. It was a voicemail. Charlemagne swiped to unlock his phone and listen.

"Oh, well that answers it. You were right. She is with her friend."

Charlemagne changed gears and pulled away from the curb to drive off.

"Apologies I was late," Charlemagne remarked. "I had an interview at the manor that didn't finish until about ten minutes ago. I knew it was almost that time of the day when the ghosts begin to cause mayhem as well, so I thought I would simply pick you up in this and drive you straight home."

"It's no big deal," Tristan remarked.

Charlemagne's phone vibrated in the cup holder. It then vibrated again.

"Oh damn," Charlemagne said. "Would you mind seeing about that message? I'm in a school zone and there's an officer ahead checking the speed."

Tristan picked up Charlemagne's phone and looked at the notifications. He read the first message and noticed it wasn't from the hotline, but an actual person.

"Hey, who's Judith?" Tristan questioned.

"Judith?" Charlemagne whispered to himself. "She's the chief scientist at Cabernet Laboratories. Why?"

"Oh snap," Tristan replied. "She's sent you a long text and it looks urgent. Apparently something bad has happened at the labs and she needs you to come right away. The test subject's escaped, or something…"

"What?" Charlemagne questioned, grabbing his phone from Tristan's hands as he continued to drive. "Oh dear…"

Charlemagne dropped his phone back into the cupholder and made an immediate left on the road heading into downtown Allabrese. Tristan took Charlemagne's phone back into his hand as it continued to vibrate.

"You've got pending calls," Tristan explained. "From the hotline – lots of dispatches."

"They'll have to wait," Charlemagne replied, focusing on the road. "A loose spirit at Cabernet Laboratories could be more destructive and threatening than a ghost by the diner, now wouldn't it?"

"Fair enough," Tristan replied, putting the phone back into the cupholder.

Charlemagne sped along the freeway east before exiting into the parking lot where sirens were flashing by the front entrance. Charlemagne could see ambulances, a fire truck and police cruisers parked. He stopped the car nearby, shifted gears and brought up the parking brake before exiting.

"Wait here," Charlemagne warned Tristan.

Tristan looked at him as he opened his door and stepped out. Charlemagne went around to the back of the truck to get his gear. He then started to walk towards the main entrance, pointing at Tristan with a serious glance.

"I won't warn you again," Charlemagne said. "You don't know what violent and cruel thing could be in there. Stay by the car."

Charlemagne entered the front lobby of the laboratories. A large crowd stood around consisting of the entire staff as well as paramedics, police officers, and firefighters. The emergency alarm bell rang loudly, and the ground was mixed with broken glass and puddles. Charlemagne walked forward to two police officers interrogating scientists.

"What's happened?" Charlemagne questioned.

"Mr. Cabernet, we're sorry," a man said.

"Excuse me, Mr. Cabernet," a police officer remarked. "If you could back off, I'm in the middle of asking some questions."

"To hell with your questions! This is my property! Where is the spirit?!"

Charlemagne marched past them and came down the corridor towards the service elevator.

"You there, open this elevator," Charlemagne remarked at a security officer.

"Yes, sir," the man said.

Charlemagne entered the elevator and came down to the sub-basement. He then exited the elevator and looked around the hall. It was dark and the sole light were flashing orange lamps scattered along the corridor. The security officer left him on his own to go down the corridor to where the doors to the containment laboratory were wide open. Paramedics exited with a woman on a stretcher. A security officer behind them followed to the elevator. Charlemagne entered the room and looked around.

Additional paramedics were around the room, attending to more staff inside. The entire glass of the vat had shattered into pieces on the floor. Dr. Lambert was nearby, being seen to by paramedics helping her onto a stretcher.

"Judith!" Charlemagne remarked, rushing over to her.

Charlemagne caught up as the paramedics began to evacuate her. His hands trembled as he grabbed hold of the stretcher with one hand and noticed the large fragment of metal in her thigh.

"My God," Charlemagne remarked.

"It's… it's gone," she said in a weak voice.

"Don't you worry, love," Charlemagne said, letting go of the stretcher as he continued to walk with them. "The paramedics will get you to the hospital on the double."

"Find her!" Judith remarked as she was brought to the elevator. "Find her!"

Charlemagne stood back as the doors closed. He frowned and readied the cannon as he returned to the containment room. There, he switched on his goggles and looked around.

"Mr. Cabernet!" a voice yelled from behind.

Charlemagne turned around to look at a warm figure walking towards him. He turned off his goggles and looked at the security officer.

"I'm the shift supervisor, Mr. Cabernet. I've come to let you know that the fusion reactor chamber is safe and that the entire building is on lockdown until further note on order of Mr. Richard Huxley. We've evacuated the staff either out of the building or into the main foyer."

Charlemagne looked at the officer. He wore a brown tactical shirt with a ballistic vest overtop. He also wore brown cargo trousers and steel-toe boots. He had short brown hair, moustache, and blue eyes.

"Thank you, son," Charlemagne replied. "Tell me, do you have any idea of what happened here?"

"I'm afraid not," the officer replied. "There's no closed-circuit footage of this room, but we do have cameras in the corridors. We could review that, if you'd like."

"Please."

"When I heard the alarms go off, I was sure that it had something to do with the Medici thugs – I never imagined something like this."

"The Medici family are the last of our concern at the moment."

"Of course, sir."

The officer paused for a moment as he listened to his earpiece. He then brought his hand to the shoulder remote microphone.

"Copy that, I'm with him."

"Mr. Cabernet," the officer said.

"Yes," Charlemagne replied as he continued to look at the room.

"Chief Phillips is here, and we think it'd be best if you spoke with him."

"Oh damn," Charlemagne remarked. "Very well, take me upstairs then please."

The officer escorted Charlemagne back to the elevator and upstairs. Charlemagne then walked back into the foyer where Chief Phillips was.

"Charles," the chief said, stepping forward.

"Chief," Charlemagne greeted.

“What the hell happened here?”

“That’s what I’m trying to figure out,” he replied. “I’ve been here for less than ten minutes but came as soon as I got word of a specimen downstairs breaking loose and escaping.”

“What specimen?” the chief questioned.

“A ghost, sir.”

“A ghost… Of course it was,” the chief replied, shaking his head. “I must extend my congratulations to you, Charles. You were truly right about the Elmwood case. You truly were right, weren’t you…?”

Charlemagne extended a serious face to the chief and his sarcastic tone.

“I have to let it be said,” Phillips continued. “I know that this company is rotten and up to something. I don’t know what. All I do know is that these ‘ghosts’ have been too suspicious and sudden to be called a natural phenomenon.”

“The reputation of my company is solid,” Charlemagne defended. “And if I hear another bit of slander about this corporation, I’ll have a very strong word with Mayor Grayson about it. I’m insulted that you’d believe my company would be behind a conspiracy like that. People were hurt today – people are always in danger when these disturbances occur, and I’m the only one that’s been there to do anything.”

“Yes, bravo,” Phillips replied. “You’ve never really been one to consider the safety of others, however. Have you? I should arrest you on grounds of contempt, but to be frank, it wouldn’t be worth the time filing all that paperwork.”

The chief unclipped a beeping pager from his belt, looked at it, and then looked back at Charlemagne.

“If you’ll excuse me, I have a vice investigation that needs to be seen to. There are bigger concerns with another crime family than with yours.”

"Give my greetings to Giovanni then," Charlemagne replied.

"Mr. Cabernet?" a familiar voice said.

Charlemagne looked behind him to see the same security officer from earlier.

"Yes," Charlemagne said, looking at him.

"This is Dr. Samuelson. She said she was in the room when the… spirit escaped."

"Oh, thank you. Please, doctor. Do tell me what occurred," Charlemagne said, taking out his notebook.

"It was horrible. I thought we were all dead," the doctor told him. "We were conducting tests when all of the sudden the pressure inside the chamber started to build. The glass then shattered and plasma ejected before we could hit the emergency suspension button. Then, it was gone. Nothing else."

"CCTV footage didn't pick up anything except the glass of the front lobby shattering," the officer added.

"Very well," Charlemagne replied. "Thank you, doctor. Thank you, security. The building can remain on lockdown and the facility can be shut down until tomorrow morning. I'll send word that the rest of staff can be sent home."

"Understood, sir."

Charlemagne made his way through the atrium and back outside. He brought the cannon to the back of the truck, removed the rest of his gear and then slammed the tail gate closed.

"Is everything okay?" Tristan questioned with concern.

"No," Charlemagne replied. "Everything is not okay. The ghost I captured at the library escaped. It's long gone."

"Oh…" Tristan replied, looking around.

"I'm going to take you home so I can follow up on these pending calls. Get in the truck," Charlemagne said. "I'm late as it is already."

Charlemagne entered the truck and picked up his phone. He looked at the five pending calls before turning the keys to ignite the engine. He then put his phone away, shifted gears, and lowered the parking brake to get moving.

Act 4, Scene 3

Charlemagne crossed the penultimate address on his list. He then took a deep breath and looked at the last address on his list, 1489 Dawson Road. Charlemagne lowered the parking brake and pulled out from the curb he was parked at. He made his way onto the freeway, driving towards the bridge before turning right to come into the suburbs.

1489 Dawson Road, also known as the Dawson Estate, was a three-story Victorian home built at the start of the last century. Charlemagne parked in front of the hedges, which itself was in front of the property's tall steel fence. It was past sunset and dark now. Charlemagne looked at the house with doubt as he turned the car off. He then got out and went to get his things with no particular rush.

Once Charlemagne had everything, he came to the gate of the house and pushed against it. It creaked open for him to continue along the path towards the steps going to the front entrance. Charlemagne went up each step and then came to the top. He lowered the cannon onto the ground and knocked on the door.

"Paranormal Investigations," Charlemagne announced for the fifth time today.

Charlemagne waited for half a minute before he heard chains being removed and locks being unlocked. The door then slowly opened to be left ajar as an old woman looked out.

"Yes?" the woman asked in the softest, but also fragile voice.

"Mrs. Dawson, I presume," Charlemagne greeted. "It's me, Mr. Cabernet. I apologize for the long delay, but I've been tied up all over the county…"

"Mr. Cabernet?" the woman questioned. "What are you doing here at this hour?"

"I'm sorry? I do believe that you, or someone at this address, called for my services," Charlemagne explained.

Charlemagne then heard a voice behind the door. The woman was whisked away and the door was closed. Charlemagne heard the sound of more locks and chains being taken off before the door opened wide. Principal Phillips stood in front of her mother with an apologetic look.

"Hello, Charles," she said.

"Sabrina," Charlemagne greeted.

"Yes, it was me who phoned for you," Mrs. Phillips said. "Please, come in."

Charlemagne entered the house, coming into the circular foyer with its black and white floor and carved wooden walls painted white. The stairway upstairs spanned around the wall, and there were various archways leading into different rooms from the foyer. The house had smell of must and dust. Picture frames were lined against the wall, most with old pictures, and some with newer pictures of Mrs. Phillips and her husband, Police Chief Phillips, and children, Aaron, Emilie, and Lila.

Charlemagne looked at Sabrina Phillips. She was dressed in a black and white dress, and her skin was as white as always and hair as black as darkness. Her eyes were green like the small emerald gem in the gold locket around her neck. Her mother, Mrs. Dawson, was a skinny and fragile old woman who spoke in equally fragile, but soft voice. Her hair was white and short. She wore a pink robe and had a slight hunch. She was also very short and had grey eyes.

"Sabrina, what is he doing in the house?" Mrs. Dawson asked.

"Please, mama," Sabrina replied. "He is here to help and investigate that apparition you had."

"I had no apparition," the woman denied. "I saw her with my own two eyes. She was here."

"She saw something?" Charlemagne questioned.

"My mother claimed to have seen her mother, 'young and beautiful,' in an old Victorian dress. She came down and apparently cared for her before leaving. All of this in the span of an hour or so."

"I did see her!" Mrs. Dawson complained, raising a hand up before leaving.

"I see, and did you see anything?" Charlemagne questioned Mrs. Phillips.

"No, I arrived about twenty minutes later," Mrs. Phillips replied, rubbing her eyes and temples. "I had a nap after work and came around about five o'clock."

"Are you alright?"

"Yes, it's just… I've had a very long day and all of this has been too much for me," Sabrina replied. "And I hate seeing her like this."

"Dementia, right?" Charlemagne asked.

"Yes."

"And you doubt that she saw your grandmother?" he asked.

"A bit, but not really," Sabrina replied. "You see, you know how it is with us Dawsons. We're known for being a bit… odd, and with all that's happened in this town in the last month or so, I had to call you to be sure. So please, can you just investigate and look around? A part of me wants to believe, and another fears that her dementia is getting worse."

"Of course," Charlemagne replied. "I'll do my best to see what's going on."

"Thank you, Charles. Is it okay if I leave you with her? I've been here long enough as it and have to return home to see the kids."

"Yes, of course. I understand," Charlemagne said. "Go right ahead."

"Thank you, Charles," Mrs. Phillips said, walking over to the living room. "Ma, I'm leaving now, but Charlemagne de la Cabernet is here and is going to look around the house. Is that okay?"

"No!" Mrs. Dawson objected.

"Okay," she replied, turning back to face Charlemagne. "Let me know what you find, please. Don't let her upset you too much. She's docile and can just be verbally aggressive."

"That's quite alright," Charlemagne replied. "Take care."

Mrs. Phillips left, leaving Charlemagne to walk into the living room. The room was colored in a bright pink with puffy white couches, a white fur carpet, and many teacup saucers hung against the pink-white wall. A large flat screen TV sat opposite the couch, and there was also a recliner chair where Mrs. Dawson sat.

"What are you doing here?" Mrs. Dawson said, looking at Charlemagne.

"Your daughter called me," Charlemagne explained. "She said you saw your mother. Can you tell me about that?"

"I did see her. Oh, it was the most wonderful thing," Mrs. Dawson said with a calm face as she reminisced. "She came down from the stairs in her lovely summer dress, stood right where you are now and spoke to me in her soothing voice. She then came and knelt down, touching my cheek with her soft hands to ask if I was alright."

Charlemagne entered the living room and sat down.

"And how did you react to this? Didn't you consider it strange to see your mother after all these years?" Charlemagne asked, taking out his notebook and pen to write notes.

"Of course I did, but she was real! She wasn't some sort of ghost – I felt her touch me with her warm hands and look at me with her green eyes. She brought me my favorite soup – leek and spinach vegetable soup, and she hugged with her warm embrace. Oh… it was surreal, yes, but it *was* real."

"Right," Charlemagne replied, taking notes.

"Oh, where are my manners? Mrs. Dawson said. "Can I offer you a hot cup of tea? Perhaps a slice of cake?"

"Oh no, love," Charlemagne replied. "I'm good, really."

"Nonsense, it's no trouble for me. I'll bring you a hot cup right away."

Mrs. Dawson stood up and left the room. Charlemagne continued to take notes before he sighed to himself. The woman later returned with a tray and a single cup of tea. She froze at the archway as she and Charlemagne looked to each other. She had a surprised look to her face.

"Oh, what are you doing here?" Mrs. Dawson asked. "How did you get into the house?"

"Mrs. Dawson… your daughter, Sabrina, let me in," Charlemagne explained again.

"Oh, I wish she could have told me she was bringing a guest over otherwise I wouldn't have made this cup of tea just for myself."

"No worries, ma'am," Charlemagne expressed, standing up. "If you'll excuse, I need to go use the washroom."

"Yes, yes," Mrs. Dawson replied, setting the tray down on the coffee table before sitting down again.

Charlemagne left the room and entered the foyer again. He produced a handheld scanner from his belt and began to press some buttons on it. He then lowered his goggles and turned them on. Charlemagne began to look around the foyer before entering the next room over, which was a dining room. He then came into the kitchen and then a study looking out to the porch and garden. From the study, he entered a library, and from the library, he entered a conservatory for music and then a conservatory for plants. Charlemagne eventually returned to the foyer where he looked to the stairs leading upwards.

The second floor consisted of various bedrooms. Charlemagne paused in a corridor as he looked at various pictures along the wall from over the years. There were additional pictures of Sabrina and her family, in addition to herself when she was younger and her sisters, her uncle, Mortimer Dawson, and various other figures from over the years, including Sabrina's grandmother, Curtia Dawson.

Charlemagne paused at this photo as he looked at the rare colorized photo from the turn of the century. In the frame was a beautiful woman in a white summer dress, looking to the camera with her tame blue eyes. Charlemagne frowned at the picture before continuing onwards. He eventually found stairs leading to the third floor attic.

The stairs upwards creaked with every step leading to the low ceiling room. The attic was messier than the basement at Cabernet Manor. Charlemagne looked at all the many antiques, bookcases and furniture hidden behind dusty white sheets. He passed a wardrobe that he noticed to be open. Charlemagne approached the wardrobe, opened the other door and looked inside. He then began to go through each outfit before stopping at some dresses. Charlemagne looked at them briefly before closing the wardrobe. He then turned around to look at his reflection in a mirror hanging by the ceiling.

Charlemagne shivered as he felt a breeze of wind hit him on the shoulder. He quickly turned with his gadgets to look around for something, but there was nothing to be seen. Charlemagne returned to the ground floor and instead of speaking to Mrs. Dawson, he silently left with his things and returned to his truck.

At his truck, Charlemagne retrieved his cellphone and phoned Sabrina Dawson, going straight to her voicemail to leave a message.

"Hello, Sabrina, it's Charlemagne. I investigated your mother's house thoroughly, and I must say that I do not believe she truly saw an apparition. I'm sorry to inform you of this."

Charlemagne left the message there and then put his things in the rear of the truck. He then came to the front of his car to step inside and write in his notebook to write the same conclusion. Charlemagne then put his notebook on the dashboard and ran his hand through his moist grey hair before turning the keys to leave.

There were seldom lights lit at Cabernet Manor. Charlemagne drove up the causeway to the front of the mansion where he saw Diana opening the door with her spare key. She paused as she looked at Charlemagne get out of the truck, and the two met at the top of the steps for Charlemagne to open the door instead.

"What are you doing out so late still?" Charlemagne quietly greeted, turning the key.

"I could say the same with you," Diana replied. "Where've you been?"

"I was out working," Charlemagne said, looking at his watch. "I suppose it is not that late. You're still an hour to your curfew. Did you eat? I'm famished."

"Yeah, I ate," Diana replied as they entered the foyer. "I would have been back sooner, but my friend's dad only just got home. He was nice enough to drive me though."

"Why didn't you call?" Charlemagne questioned.

Diana shrugged as the two of them were about to split up to either staircase.

"Do you know Moira's dad, Mr. Macmillan?" Diana questioned.

"I'm familiar with him," Charlemagne replied. "Go on."

"Well, he was out late because he was investigating a serious crime that happened on the other side of town – a homicide."

"A murder?" Charlemagne asked.

"*Murders*," Diana corrected. "Mr. Macmillan was pretty frustrated about the whole thing – didn't know how it was done."

"Is that so…" Charlemagne questioned, pausing for a moment.

"Yeah, it was pretty intimidating to hear about it… I mean, I'm used to it all being from Keswick, but still – I thought this town was supposed to be safe. I never expected anything like that around here… Other than the fact that you were almost killed, I mean."

Charlemagne watched Diana as she left after those final words. She went up the stairs and disappeared into the other wing of the house, leaving Charlemagne in the foyer with a pensive look. He finally woke up and went to his bedroom to get changed, coming out showered and in his traditional grey pinstripe linin suit. He then went to the kitchen to have a quick meal.

Act 4, Scene 4

Charlemagne walked to his study from the kitchen and sat down. He turned on his computer and immediately started to hack into the police servers again using the same device that appeared to still be on the back of Chief Phillip's computer.

The computer was awoken from Charlemagne's desk and he began to search for the most recent reports in the system by Eugene Macmillan. He opened the report and began to read into the narrative:

'On October 27, 2017, at approximately 1705 hours, the Nattau County Police Department was dispatched by emergency services to respond to a homicide reported at the Medici Manor on 27 Palatine Lane.

Constable H. ALEXANDER was first on-scene and briefed by Dino MEDICI, Security Lead of the site and nephew to the victims. At approximately 1720 hours, Constable M. CLARK, Constable L. TRUSCOTT and Captain E. MACMILLAN arrived and were briefed by Constable ALEXANDER. The victims of the homicide were identified as Giovanni MEDICI and Bianca Medici in the master bedroom of the house. At this time, the Office of the Chief Medical Examiner was notified to further investigate the cause of death in detail. Captain MACMILLAN investigated the surroundings and found an emptied Bodeo Model 1889 with the victim, Giovanni MEDICI, which did not match 9mm cases found near the bed, suggesting another weapon at the crime scene and third person of interest. Captain MACMILLAN attempted to gain permission to search the grounds but was denied by Dino MEDICI. According to Dino MEDICI, he was unaware Giovanni MEDICI's return to the house as he had been missing since July. In addition, access to the master bedroom and other personal quarters in the mansion are under restricted access with Dino MEDICI. He was unsure of how any perpetrator could have entered the manor and by extension, the master bedroom. CCTV footage disclosed to the Nattau Police Department show no intruders on the property nor suspicious persons entering the house over the last twenty-four hours. Police inquired into the identities of individuals with access to the master bedroom and was told by Dino MEDICI produced the following list: Nero MEDICI (deceased), Giovanni MEDICI, Bianca MEDICI, Arturo MEDICI, Bruno MEDICI, Mercutio MEDICI, Italo MEDICI, and Dino MEDICI. Police also inquired into the alibi of Dino MEDICI, however, he had not been present on the site when Giovanni MEDICI until he himself was notified by Arturo MEDICI about the murder. In addition, Arturo MEDICI was unavailable to provide a testimony at the time of this investigation. Italo MEDICI has been confirmed to be in Italy at the present-time, serving a sentence in Federal Prison.

At approximately 2010 hours, Captain MACMILLAN stood down. Nattau Police Department is waiting for forensic experts and a coroner to retrieve the corpses at Medici Manor. This report will remain 'in progress' until then.'

Charlemagne finished reading the report before opening the pictures attached to the file. The first picture showed a man in a black suit, on the ground with open blue eyes and a bullet wound through the chest. He had dark black hair and olive skin tone. The second picture showed a blonde woman in a green dress laying atop of the bed with her arms stretched apart. She had a bullet wound through the forehead with blood stain seeping down her face.

"My God," Charlemagne muttered to himself. "Those poor children… parentless."

Charlemagne looked to the next picture, which showed bullet holes in a wall and pillar. There was also an image of the Bodeo Model 1889 revolver and some bullet cases on the floor. The final images taken were of the hands of both victims. Giovanni's was dirtier and displayed that he had fired the revolver. Bianca had clean hands. Charlemagne went through all of the intel available once more, downloaded a copy, and then disconnected himself from the police servers.

From his study, Charlemagne took his coat as it had started to rain and went to the garage via the freight elevator. He then walked to his sedan and entered it to drive out to the Medici home. From the coast opposite of Allabrese, across the bridge, through downtown and towards the east side of the county along the freeway, and down south, Charlemagne found himself near fields of agriculture before coming close to the vineyard countryside close to the villa known as Medici Mansion.

The home represented a legacy of the Medici family since their arrival in 1870 in what was formerly territory on the outskirts of the settlement, but became incorporated in the county in the turn of the century. Charlemagne pulled over a couple of yards from the mansion property and behind a large shrub to conceal his vehicle.

Charlemagne got his forensics briefcase from the back of his sedan. He closed the trunk and started to make his way towards the mansion gates. He stopped less than halfway to look at the mansion and think.

"Perhaps if I'm honest, they'll just let me in," Charlemagne expressed to himself. "Or perhaps, they'd kill me to finish the job and avenge those incarcerated because of me."

Charlemagne diverged from the path down the road and came into the bushes of the vineyard. He started to walk along the outskirts of the mansion before starting to walk towards the outer walls again. Along the wall, he found some vines near an arch and metal gate. Charlemagne slid the briefcase through the gate before he grabbed some vines to climb over the wall. He came to the top of the wall and rested his arms over the top, hiding himself as he saw two gangsters below on the other side, walking past.

"Are those cops gone?" one of them asked.

"Off the property," the other replied. "They wanted to maintain presence, but Dino wanted them gone. He told them we'd maintain the site secure."

Both of the gangsters were dressed in the standard blue pinstripe suit, but with additional black coats and hats to protect themselves from the rain. Each of them were also carrying flashlights, pointed in front of them.

"With *Il Duce* dead, who is leading us anymore? What's going to happen to family? The business? We're done, I tell you. We're ruined."

Charlemagne watched as the guards walked off before climbing up and then over the wall. He quickly grabbed the briefcase and then proceeded down the opposite way of the gravel path. Charlemagne reached a set of staircase going down into a small alcove in the side of the house where he found a wooden door. He hid in the darkness of the alcove as another patrol passed by.

Once the guard passed, Charlemagne stepped back into the light and turned to face the door. He attempted to open the door knob, but it was locked. Charlemagne then knelt down and opened his briefcase to produce a screwdriver and hairpin. He then inserted the hair pin in the lock and proceeded to tap into the lock to unlock the door.

"Cheers, Diana," Charlemagne whispered as he turned the lock.

Charlemagne put his tools away before opening the door, stepping inside and locking the door behind him. He paused for a moment as he looked at the darkness ahead and produced a flashlight to see. He was in a basement corridor with grey stone brick walls on either side and flagstone floor at his feet. The ceiling was arched with lamps spread along the center leading forward. The corridor intersected in the middle and made a left at the end. There was a door to the right of the corner as well. Charlemagne made his way forward, turned to face the right and shined his light into the dark corridor.

Barrels were lined along the right-side of the corridor with empty space along the left. The dripping of water could be heard as well. Charlemagne faced the room with focused eyes as his ears twitched with the sound of light metal hitting stone. He shined his light around with a feeling as if he was being watched. Charlemagne continued forward, turned left and then went right as he found a set of stairs going up.

The stone stairs turned and led to an open door. Charlemagne opened the door and found himself in the regal red corridors of the Medici home. He continued to the left, walking down and finding himself at a junction. Charlemagne looked both ways before going right and coming to an archway leading into what appeared to be the main foyer.

The main foyer had a set of staircases going upwards, which was where Charlemagne went. He arrived at another corridor that went both ways. Charlemagne chose to go to the right, walking down and choosing either between another set of stairs going up or going around the corner to a dead-end with a choice of two doors. Charlemagne decided to retrace his steps and go the other route. There, he was able to turn right and find a door at the end of the corridor with police tape over it.

Charlemagne walked over to the door and removed the tape. He then tried to open the door, but it was locked. Next to the door was a biometric panel with the brand name at the bottom, 'Zimmerman Corps.' Charlemagne lowered his briefcase, opened it, and took out an ultraviolet lamp. He began to shine the light around the door, looking around the surface before putting the light away. He then took out a screwdriver and began to pry the security panel open and fumble with the wires until he heard a click from the door.

"Simple," Charlemagne sneered as he opened the door. "They should have bought from Cabernet."

Charlemagne pushed the door open, put his screwdriver away and then picked up his briefcase to enter the master bedroom.

Inside, letter markers were left on the ground alongside blankets over the corpses. Charlemagne closed the door behind him before he got a better look through the moonlight. The room had a large king-sized bed in the middle rear where Bianca Medici was laying atop. In front of the bed was a divan, and in front of the divan was a rug with the corpse of Giovanni Medici. The middle of the room, where the bed and end tables were, was raised on a small platform with pillars at the corner. The outer room had a walk-in closet, door leading to a bathroom, wardrobe, dressers, desk and mirror.

Charlemagne knelt down to uncover Giovanni's body. He was just as he was in the picture, but in greater detail. He wore an expensive black suit with a black dress shirt, crimson tie, and black dress shoes. Dried up blood could be seen around the bullet wound. Charlemagne stood up and brought his briefcase atop of the dresser behind the body. From his case, he produced a scalpel and set of tweezers. He then put on some large-sized blue latex gloves before taking his tools to kneel down.

The scalpel cut into the string tying the button to the black shirt, allowing Charlemagne to expose the chest and by extension, the wound in the left pectoral. Charlemagne took an alcohol tampon wipe and cleaned the skin from the blood. He then took the tweezers to the wound to dig out the bullet before dropping it into his glove. Charlemagne then picked up one of the 10.35mm cartridges to try and put the two together. He then brought both the cartridge and bullet back to his briefcase to set the two into separate transparent bags.

Afterwards, Charlemagne returned to pick up the revolver. He opened the chamber, but there was nothing inside. Charlemagne set the gun down and looked forward, towards a chair facing the body of one of the pillars. He noticed some bullet holes behind the chair. Charlemagne walked forward to examine the wall before going back to his suitcase to retrieve a chisel. He then returned to the holes and began to chisel around them to search for one of the bullets lodged inside. The bullet dropped onto the ground for Charlemagne to pick up alongside one of the 9mm cartridges near the chair. Charlemagne brought both back to the dresser and set them onto plastic bags.

Charlemagne began to dust the cartridges for fingerprints, finding a pair each for him to copy. He then went to each body to take their fingerprints before returning to compare the results to the one's collected. Only one of the cartridges matched with one of Giovanni's fingerprints. Neither Bianca nor Giovanni's fingerprints matched with the print on the 9mm cartridge. Charlemagne set the bullet found in the wall with the 10.35mm cartridge and the bullet found in Giovanni with the 9mm cartridge. He then walked over to the bed and looked down at the blanket covering Bianca Medici.

Mrs. Medici had a grim final appearance with an open mouth and saggy open eyes. Eyeliner was smeared down from her eyes as though she was crying in her final moments. Charlemagne looked at the wound in her head, the crack in her cranium and imagined the bullet inwards. He collected the specimen and brought it back to the dresser. It was a match for the bullet originating from the 9mm cartridge.

Charlemagne began to search the room for additional evidence to examine. He walked around the right-side of the bed before going around to the right. Charlemagne noticed a phone atop of the counter and picked it up. He looked at all phone numbers listed, representing calls made and received. He brought the phone back to his briefcase and began to write all of the ones over the last twenty-four hours.

After Charlemagne had finished writing the phone numbers down, he returned to where Giovanni was and stood in front of the corpse. He then turned around with a laser pointer and pointed the laser towards the bullet holes in the wall. The trajectory passed through the chair.

"Straight through, no blood around at a point-blank shot," Charlemagne muttered to himself. "Either Giovanni was firing at a *ghost*, or..."

Charlemagne paused at those words.

"Or he has terrible aim."

Charlemagne walked over to the chair and pointed the laser back towards the corpse, or where Giovanni would have been standing before he was shot. Afterwards, Charlemagne began to look around at all the windows and examined them. He then returned to the dresser to note his findings before looking at the four phone numbers found on the home phone over the last day. Charlemagne then took out his own phone to search for each number on his internet browser. Only two of the numbers came back and were connected with Medici Construction. The other two were unknown.

Charlemagne noted the location of two of the numbers before looking at all his notes. He left the bullets and cartridges in the plastic bags and atop the dresser before closing his briefcase. With a sigh, he picked up his briefcase and started to leave. Charlemagne made his way back downstairs, and back towards the door leading into the basement. He set foot onto the stone floor and started to go back to the door he entered from when he began to hear the moans of something, or someone nearby.

The noise was not distant. Charlemagne paused where he was to listen more closely. It was the sound of someone crying. He looked around with his flashlight, shining it at a nearby door. Charlemagne walked over and pressed his ear to the door. He then lowered a hand to the doorknob to open the door.

Inside the small room was a short countertop and two chairs with monitors and keyboards atop. Some of the computer screens were blank, while others had small green and red text running along the black backgrounds. At the chair farthest, with both feet atop of the chair so that he had his knees to his chest was a young boy with his face buried into his legs. The boy looked to Charlemagne.

"Arturo," Charlemagne greeted.

"Who are you?" the boy replied.

"My name is Charlemagne Cabernet," Charlemagne replied.

"What are you doing here? Get out!"

"You were reported missing," Charlemagne said instead. "Does anybody know you're down here?"

Arturo didn't reply. He instead buried his head back into his legs. The boy looked similar to his father. He had tanned skin as well and fine black hair. Although, in contrast to Giovanni, Arturo had a strong jaw and nose similar to his mother. He was dressed in jeans, a collared-shirt and dark blue zip hoodie. He also wore black sneakers.

"I'm not here to hurt you, dear boy," Charlemagne said in a soft voice. "I'm only here to investigate what happened here tonight. I understand that it may be hard, but you need to get into contact with whoever is in charge of you and your brothers."

"Nobody is anymore."

Charlemagne continued to look at the boy before shifting his eyes to the keyboard in front of him. Near the keyboard was something hidden near the neck of the computer monitor. Charlemagne brought his flashlight towards it to see it to be a pistol. His eyes widened and he instantly lowered the light away as he continued to look at Arturo with the dim light emitting from the monitor to the left being the sole source of light. Charlemagne looked at the monitor and read the lines. Each line resembled a separate electronic panel within the house and the most recent activity. On the monitor next to this one was a map of the entire grounds with symbols at each entrance.

The master bedroom door, for example, was displaying as malfunctioning due to Charlemagne's tampering. Charlemagne read each line over again, going so far as to earlier this evening and focusing on the master bedroom. At approximately the time of when the body was discovered, it displayed Dino Medici as who unlocked the door. Charlemagne looked at the boy as he read who was prior.

"You killed them," Charlemagne quietly said. "Didn't you?"

"No, it wasn't me," Arturo denied. "I didn't do it. I... He... won't get out of my head!"

"What do you mean?" Charlemagne replied, sitting down in the chair next to Arturo. "Who won't get out of your head?"

"You wouldn't understand – you wouldn't believe me! I'm crazy! I'm crazy and I know it! This is all a dream... a terrible nightmare! I didn't kill my parents! No!"

Arturo began to cry again. All Charlemagne could do was look back at the child.

"I'm going to wake up... I'm going to wake up, and they're still going to be alive."

"You're... You're not in a dream, Arturo," Charlemagne replied.

"Shut up! Don't speak! Don't speak!" Arturo shouted at him, kicking Charlemagne in the knees.

Charlemagne wasn't bothered by the kicking, but did have worried eyes towards the gun near Arturo. Charlemagne took a deep breath before looking back at Arturo. Both were silent as Medici continued to cry. Charlemagne simply remained where he was until the boy calmed himself down and ceased crying.

Eventually Charlemagne started to realize that the boy had his head to the side with eyes looking to the pistol on the table. Charlemagne looked back at the gun and then to Arturo.

"You're going to call the police on me, aren't you," Arturo said.

"I haven't even thought of the police," Charlemagne replied in the same soft voice. "All I'm thinking of is getting you back to your cousin, Dino."

"You know the truth, though," Arturo continued. "You know it was me."

"Was it you?"

"I don't know," Arturo replied with a weak voice, burying his face back into his knees. "I watched it happen with my own eyes and own hands around the gun. I remember it all in such detail, and I saw their bodies in their room, but I can't believe that I could have done it. It all feels like it was just a really bad dream, but I feel the coldness of this room on my skin and I hear the water dripping in the cellar behind me. I hear your voice and I have my thoughts. I'm awake and this has all happened, and that is perhaps what is most terrifying. I am awake and this is real. What do I do?"

"I believe you should see Dino," Charlemagne repeated, "and get some rest."

"Rest?" Arturo replied as though offended, raising his head up to look at Charlemagne. "I don't want to sleep. How can I sleep after something like this had just happened? I murdered my parents! My own hands pulled the trigger and they're gone forever now!"

"Easy," Charlemagne responded, hushing him.

"I didn't even do it, Mr. Cabernet. I swear," Arturo began to say, crying. "It wasn't me. He forced me to do. He possessed me and made me do it."

"Who?"

Arturo was silent and didn't reply.

"The Immortal One," Arturo said. "The one that was supposed to be dead but isn't. He told me I could be a better leader than my father. He told me I would be happier if he was gone. I don't feel happier... I feel horrible. How can anyone ever kill?"

"I need a name," Charlemagne insisted.

"My nonno," Arturo answered.

"Nero?" Charlemagne questioned.

"He tricked me. Everything he ever said to me is a damn lie. I feel so stupid."

Charlemagne's eyes wandered the room as he thought. He also grew cold. His eyes looked into the darkness, searching as though he was being watched.

"You probably don't even believe me. I know I'm crazy," Arturo said.

"I believe you," Charlemagne said. "In all honesty, I can believe you. I knew your grandfather, and he was the very definition of evil."

"How can you believe me?"

"Because I've seen some very improbable things over the last two months, and to believe that Nero could manipulate an innocent child like you, would not be the craziest of them."

"What do I do then? I feel horrible. My parents are dead, and.... and... they'll be looking for a killer. My fingerprints are on the gun, and... I kind of did do it. It was me that pulled the trigger. I saw with my own eyes. I heard the gun shot – I watched it all."

"Except that was not you in the right mind nor even free will, was it?"

Arturo shook his head.

"Nobody else would believe me like you do though," Arturo said depressingly, wiping his forehead.

"Come," Charlemagne said, standing up and offering his hand. "Step out of the darkness for a start and let's get you some water. You must be feverish – being feverish won't help you feel better."

"I want revenge," Arturo instead said, looking up to Charlemagne. "I hate him more than anything. He took them from me," he added, eyes watering. "All I want is revenge."

"I'll ensure that his spirit isn't free," Charlemagne simply offered.

Arturo stood up and Charlemagne opened the door behind him. The two stepped out and Charlemagne took the boy upstairs. Arturo held his chin down as he walked with Charlemagne. The two came to the foyer, and from the foyer they walked into a room underneath the stairway. It was a room without any windows, but various desks around. Several gangsters could be seen inside.

"Arturo!" one of them said, turning to him. "Charlemagne!"

All three of the gangsters wore the standard blue suit, but without the blazer. The one that shouted stood behind a table with documents piled around and had his sleeves rolled up. He also had a beard across his chin and thick, long black hair. The others were behind desks in chairs and computers in front of them.

All three of the gangsters took out their firearms and pointed them to Charlemagne.

"No! Stop!" Arturo yelled. "Put those away! No more death!"

"Huh?" the one with sleeves rolled up questioned.

"He came here to help," Arturo explained. "He also found me, and I don't need you to make a big deal of it. Dino... not after what happened."

Dino nodded and lowered his weapon.

"My parents are dead," Arturo said.

"And we're doing all we can to find out who killed them," Dino replied, walking over to him and kneeling in front of him.

Arturo hugged him as he started to cry again. Dino comforted him. The others simply tried to ignore the sorrow in the room. They looked remorseful. Dino pried Arturo from him and put a hand on his shoulder.

"What is Mr. Cabernet doing here?" Dino asked Arturo.

"He came to help," Arturo said.

"Help? Why?"

"Because the matters in which Giovanni and Bianca died were suspicious," Charlemagne explained. "And it is my belief that they met their demise because of paranormal circumstances."

"Are you insane?"

"Listen to him!" Arturo pleaded. "He's not!"

"Perhaps we should discuss this outside," Charlemagne suggested.

Dino nodded and left the room with Arturo and Charlemagne. They came to the front of the mansion so that they were alone. There, Charlemagne explained what he found, and Arturo confessed his part before Charlemagne warned Dino that the forensic experts would deduce that Arturo was the murderer based on his fingerprint on the 9mm cartridges and gun. Charlemagne reasoned that they could explain Arturo's biometrics being used to access the bedroom around the time the murder was to be the time when Arturo discovered the corpses, but that it would be difficult to reason why Arturo's fingerprints were on the cartridges as well as the murder weapon with no other suspects. He then went into detail about Nero Medici manipulating Arturo, which required Arturo to explain the last several months and the slow idolization he began to have for his grandfather until tonight.

"I told you to stay away from that stuff!" Dino scolded Arturo. "Nonno was a vile man that cared about nobody except himself. Why do you think our dads became the way they are? Because they didn't have a real father!"

"I'm sorry," Arturo simply said.

"What can be done to prevent the police from believing Arturo to be the real murder?" Charlemagne questioned.

"Don't worry about it, Mr. Cabernet," Dino replied, looking to him. "I'll handle it. I won't let them touch Arturo."

"Maybe they should take me away," Arturo complained with defeat.

"Nonsense," Dino said. "You've been through a lot tonight, I know, but everything is going to be okay. Do you understand?"

Arturo nodded.

"Thank you, Mr. Cabernet, for your help," Dino added, looking to him.

"My pleasure of course," Charlemagne said.

"I'll let you go on now if there's nothing else."

"Nothing else," Charlemagne assured him. "Although, I would prefer an escort off the property."

"Consider it done," Dino replied, taking his radio from his belt.

"Thank you," Charlemagne responded, looking down to Arturo with his sunken expression.

"If your grandfather shows his face around here again," Charlemagne said. "Please, call me at once."

"Yes, sir," Arturo agreed.

Act 5, Scene 1

Charlemagne pulled into the driveway of Cabernet manor, parking behind the pickup truck. He then got out and went up the steps to the front door. He entered the house and went to his lab, taking off his raincoat and sitting down at his computer. The mansion was quiet. Charlemagne turned on his computer and watched the monitor screen flicker to life

On his computer, Charlemagne wrote a report for what he had learned at the Medici home in addition to the last four cases in the same day. After he was done, he stood up and turned to the table in the middle of the room. He cleared it and went downstairs to his office to retrieve a cylindrical canister. He then brought the canister up and opened it to reveal a rolled up sheet of paper. Charlemagne unrolled the poster and set it on the table. It was a map of the entire county.

One by one, Charlemagne went through all his cases and began to pin them on the map with dressmaker pins until they were all displayed. Then, he took canvas tape and wrote the time and date the individual incidents took place. He found the following pattern: every day after 1530 hours for the last six weeks between Monday to Friday saw at least one incident. With the exception of the murder at the Medici home, each case took place within the general area surrounding downtown Allabrese.

Charlemagne looked at the map and stroked his chin. He thought and thought, but no idea came to mind. He went to bed late that night and struggled to sleep. Early next morning, he left the house and travelled to Allabrese Hospital. He parked in the parking lot and then entered the hospital through the main entrance to find a phone. He called the switchboard and asked for patient information on Judith Lambert, taking him to the intensive care unit on the second floor. There, he registered himself and entered to sit down in front of Dr. Lambert's bed where she was unconscious. Charlemagne sat for at most an hour, pondering to himself before he got up and paid a visit to the other staff members afflicted by the breakout yesterday. He spoke with all the staff and kept them company until noon when visiting hours hit a break so patients could have their lunch. Charlemagne left the hospital at this time and drove out to Cabernet Laboratories.

The parking lot of the labs were almost empty as it was a weekend. He parked in his spot at the front entrance and got out, looking across the building in the gloomy grey October skies. The shattered glass had been boarded up with long sheets of wood. A wooden door was installed in the middle of one of the sheets where the sliding doors were. Charlemagne walked over to the entrance and pressed a hand against the door. He tried to open the door, but it was locked.

Charlemagne took his car and drove around to the rear of the building and entered from there using the biometric scanners. He walked through shipping and receiving and came to the main laboratories before going down to the restricted laboratories. He entered the room where the incident took place yesterday and the ghost was being held. He looked around before walking out, spending the rest of the afternoon walking around with his hands behind his back.

Eventually, Charlemagne came to the offices where he stopped at the office of Dr. Lambert at the top floor of the office annex. Her office was at the end of a long corridor and had her name printed on the frosted glass door alongside her professional credentials. Charlemagne attempted to open the door, but it was locked. Instead of turning around and leaving, Charlemagne took out his phone and called security to have them unlock the door. He waited there for approximately five minutes until an officer arrived to unlock the door for him.

"Thank you," Charlemagne said before turning to open the door.

Charlemagne entered the office and looked inside. Bookcases were lined along the frosted glass with a desk towards the right-side. Dr. Lambert had a sofa arranged directly in front with chairs in front of her desk. Charlemagne walked towards the desk and picked up some of the photographs on the table. One was from her graduation where she was with her family. Another was a photograph of her with Charlemagne and her ex-husband. All three of them were younger and happier people. Charlemagne had yet to adopt his moustache and have his hair whiten from its light blonde color. Judith had thicker hair in the photo and wore glasses. The other man in the photo was also blonde, but in a slightly darker shade than both Charlemagne and Judith. He also wore glasses and his hair was long. He had a strong jaw and was clean shaven in this photo. Charlemagne walked around to get a better view and sat down in her seat. A laptop sat atop of the desk as well as a computer with two monitors to the right. Various folders and notebooks were on the left. Charlemagne began to go through them before finding a package envelope with his name on it that was meant to be sent out via mail. Charlemagne opened the envelope and took out a booklet of printed sheets of paper. He started to go through them one by one.

"My God," Charlemagne muttered. "That brilliant woman…"

Act 5, Scene 2

Charlemagne closed the booklet and sat back in the chair with a stunned expression. He then stood up and made his back towards the mansion as the sun set, but instead of turning into the driveway, Charlemagne continued to drive along the cliffside road where he started to drive uphill and up the mountain.

Once he was high above, he pulled into the dirt in front of a tall building with a domed roof. He got out of his car and caught a brief view of the town below before going around and up a set of staircases. Charlemagne held onto the envelope package and made his way to a pair of double doors with a sign above that read 'Nattau Observatory Center.'

Charlemagne quickly knocked on the door and waited in the chilly night. He had to knock again before the doors opened to reveal a middle-aged man, the same man in the photo with Judith and Charlemagne, but with shorter, dirty blonde hair and a thick stubble. Instead of a graduation gown, he was dressed in a graphic t-shirt and jeans.

"Charles?" the man questioned, rubbing his eyes. "Is that you?"

"Barry!" Charlemagne greeted, stepping in from the cold and walking past the man.

"What the heck are you doing up here?"

"Please, Barry. No time to explain. I need access to the Cabernet infrared satellites pointed towards the Earth," Charlemagne explained, walking towards a table and dropping the package there.

"Hello to you too," Barry said, closing the door behind him. "You're going to have to do some explaining, such as why I haven't heard from my best friend in ages."

"Oh, you know how it is," Charlemagne replied. "I've been researching and such. I'm currently working on a very important case, so please if we could save the socialization for another time, I would surely appreciate it."

"You'll have to try harder than that," Barry said, crossing his arms. "Are you okay in the least? Last I heard, you were in a hard place."

"I'm fine, Barry. I haven't been better."

"And?"

"And what more, friend? I'm in the happiest I've been over the last few months because I've welcomed into my home and under my eye two lovely orphans who have taught me the importance of children and having them, something which I missed due to my selfishness. Over the last two months, I've also landed the chance to investigate a spectacular mystery into the paranormal, and with the help of your ex-wife, I may have a breakthrough that could solve the origin of these spirits once and for all. I would love to go into greater detail, and I do apologize for seemingly forgetting about you until now, and I do wish to make up for lost time, old friend. However, now is not that time, because just yesterday, Giovanni and Bianca Medici were murdered at the hands of a vile man and pushed me to seek to end this once and for all. We have lived for centuries without such disturbances, and I know that the recent trend can be reversed if we reverse whatever it was that caused these disturbances to take place in the first place. Do you understand my urgency now?"

"Alright," Barry said. "I do."

Dr. Lambert walked over to his computer as Charlemagne looked at a large screen above the computer stations.

"It'll take a couple of hours to get the satellite into position," Barry explained. "So your urgency will have to put up with that."

"Is there any other means?"

"I'm afraid not," Barry explained. "It'll be at least six hours from where they currently are. What specifically am I looking for though?"

"Right," Charlemagne replied, opening up the package and going through the sheets of paper. "I need you to scan the county for this radiation signature."

Charlemagne slid the paper towards Barry on his desk. Barry picked up the sheet and looked at it, adjusting his glasses.

"The signature is supposedly harmless to organisms but has been hypothesized to be the trigger for all these spiritual uprisings over the last months," Charlemagne explained. "Here."

Charlemagne passed the entire package to Barry. Barry started to go through the report.

"Dr. Judith Lambert…" Barry said, reading the title page.

Charlemagne stood around as Barry went through the papers. Once he finished, he made sure each page was together in the correct order before setting it down on the desk.

"Well then, I'm certainly impressed at the work you two have been up to," Barry said. "I've heard you're quite the 'ghostbuster' down there."

"What do you think of her findings? A single particle – a quantum particle being the base of these spirits – sucking energy around them to create the cold atmosphere around them. Imagine if we could study this particle further! She's picked up on so much that I've missed – and look," Charlemagne said, picking up the report to show the picture of the spirit under ultraviolet radiation. "Look at this"

The picture demonstrated the magnetic waves surrounding the quantum particle in a bluish-purple tone on a black background. The picture made the spirit look like a wisp as Charlemagne had seen under his UV goggles at the library.

"You know," Charlemagne said. "I've enjoyed my time being able to capture these but knowing that some of these are now the trapped souls of human beings tells me that I will need to release them as soon as this crisis is over. Almost all of the spirits I've captured have been ancient spirits corresponding to Amerindians with the few exception of some wild animals such as bison and elk. I was only able to capture one Caucasoid at the Curtia Dawson Public Library, which got sent to Judith. The only problem is that it escaped…"

"How?" Barry questioned.

"I'm unsure… this happened yesterday. Most of the staff were injured, including Judith. Thankfully, nobody was killed."

"Jesus, is she okay?" Barry asked.

"I saw her today in the hospital, but she was unresponsive. She lost a lot of blood, and the ICU doctor anticipated that she'll recover in due time."

"Thank God," Barry replied. "I mean, she's my ex-wife and everything – the bane of my existence, but I still care about her."

The two entered an awkward silence.

"How has she been? Before the accident…" Barry wondered.

"She's been okay…" Charlemagne replied. "She's better than when I last saw her before I disappeared. She's made a lot of progress."

"She used to be the happiest woman alive before the miscarriage," Barry said, looking to the ceiling. "She never smiled at me ever again since what happened. She blames me."

"She blames herself," Charlemagne corrected.

"She divorced me," Barry objected.

"Because she blames herself," Charlemagne insisted. "Please, Barry. We can't have this argument again. It's the same every time."

"Sorry."

"Anyways, I don't see how she was the 'happiest woman alive' beforehand," Charlemagne said. "She was never like that around me."

"That's why she married me," Barry laughed as he looked to Charlemagne.

"The only reason she ever married you was because I introduced you to her," Charlemagne reminded him.

"And I don't regret it…" Barry said. "Even if she now has my job, and I'm exiled up here due to the restraining order."

"I'll agree that the protection order was a little over the top," Charlemagne said.

"I suppose she's a better leader than me," Barry remarked.

"You're both fine scientists. I wish both of you were working at the labs…"

Charlemagne continued to talk to Barry as the two waited for the satellite to reposition. Hours went by. Charlemagne went to the washroom and then returned to look up at the screen in tire and disgust.

"You know, sleeping will make time go by faster, even though you seem anxious – too anxious to sleep," Dr. Lambert said, standing up from his desk.

"I couldn't possibly think of going to the manor now," Charlemagne replied, looking to his friend.

"Then how about you go to one of the bedrooms in the back and sleep," Barry said. "Pick a room. There are blankets in the closets. Get some sleep, you've been up since early in the morning."

Charlemagne looked to his friend in doubt through his tired eyes.

"Right," Charlemagne said, taking a deep breath. "I ought to sleep. Goodnight then, old friend."

"Good night, Charles," Barry said, walking over to the kitchen to wash some plates.

Charlemagne stumbled to the rear of the observatory where a corridor led into a curved corridor with separate rooms that were simple with mattresses on the floor next to power outlets. Each mattress had a pillow, and at the foot of the mattresses were closets with blankets. Charlemagne laid out some blankets onto the mattress in his chosen room and then sat down. He took out his smartphone and looked at the time, quarter past twelve. He dialed Tristan's number and brought the phone to his ear. The phone went to voicemail for Charlemagne to leave a message.

"Tristan, it's me Charlemagne. I know it is late and neither you nor Diana have seen me for quite a while. I assure you both that I am fine. I am currently working at Nattau Observatory and cannot say when I'll be back. If I'm not back by Monday, I'll see to it that Mr. Huxley drives you to school. If you need anything financial-wise, please message me. Best regards, Charles."

Charlemagne turned off his phone and set it on the floor. He then yawned and climbed into bed. He lay on his side, staring at the wall before closing his eyes to try and sleep. He opened them again soon after with a worried expression, staring again at the wall through the darkness. He looked at the wall for so long, that eventually he began to notice a white glow originating from behind him.

Charlemagne turned around to look, seeing something through the crack in the door left ajar. Charlemagne got out of bed and walked over to the door, opening it to see a wisp outside his room just as in the photo. He rubbed his eyes to get a better look at the glow.

"You mustn't let him be remembered," the wisp said in a quiet feminine voice similar to Sabrina Phillip's.

"Who?" Charlemagne questioned.

The wisp led Charlemagne down the curved corridor.

"He will not be remembered. He will not be immortalized."

The wisp led Charlemagne to the end of the corridor where it phased through the end of the hall. Charlemagne walked right up the wall and brought his hands to the surface. He felt the wall, gently pushing himself against it before resting his forehead.

"Charles?" Judith said behind him.

Charlemagne turned around and his eyes opened. He looked at the wall in front of him and took a deep breath as he woke up. He was still on the mattress. His heart was beating quickly but came to rest as he sat up. Charlemagne grabbed his phone to check the time. A mere ninety minutes had passed since he had initially laid down. He laid back down and fell asleep again.

Another three hours passed before Charlemagne woke up again. He looked at the time and stood up, leaving the room with his phone. He entered the main atrium of the observatory and returned to where Barry was at his desk.

"Good morning," Charlemagne said to him.

"Wow, it's about time," Barry said, turning his neck to look at him. "Do you want some coffee? I just made a pot in the kitchen."

"Thank you," Charlemagne replied, looking at the satellite feed above. "So, it's in position?"

"And scanning," Barry said, standing up to go to the kitchen, "but we couldn't find any trace of the unique radiation signature Judith found, or any unusual energy levels across the entire county."

"Impossible," Charlemagne contested.

Dr. Lambert returned with a mug of coffee for Charlemagne.

"Thank you," Charlemagne said again.

Barry returned to his desk and sat down.

"We will have to wait until tomorrow afternoon," Charlemagne said. "Every weekday for the last several months, these spirits began to show themselves at around fifteen-hundred hours. Perhaps then we could see this unique spike."

"It would make sense," Barry replied.

"I was just hoping that we would be able to see at least something out of the ordinary at this present moment…"

"Well, I'll maintain the satellite like this for the time being and see what I can do," Barry explained. "In the meantime, I don't think there's much we can do."

Charlemagne didn't reply. He instead went silent as he looked at the ground. He remained that way for several minutes before he looked over to Barry.

"I must give my thanks to you, Barry," Charlemagne said to him. "I appreciate your help."

"What are friends for?" Barry replied.

"Yes, there's that word again…" Charlemagne remarked. "Judith said the same thing a while back. 'Friend.'"

"Well of course, Charles," Barry said in a strict tone, turning in his chair to face him. "We're your friends. Do you think just because you haven't spoken to me in two years that our friendship would just vanish? Friendship doesn't just disappear like that, especially ones that have almost lasted a lifetime. You're the one I would go to whenever I needed to vent about my family or financial troubles, and you would listen. You're the one I sat with in the dean's office because we got caught relocating the dean's car onto the roof of the clocktower. And you're the one that was there for me during the divorce."

Charlemagne didn't reply as Barry paused. He instead held a firm look on his face as he crossed his arms and looked to the other side of the room.

"I haven't forgotten either," Charlemagne finally replied in a coarse voice. "All the years we spent scheming together. Our hopes and dreams that we shared together. The moments we spent designing and inventing – turning ideas into reality. Perhaps I've been unappreciative towards the people in my life, not just in you, but also in people like Judith and Richard. You have all helped me so much with this project that I wouldn't be here without you."

"And there's nothing we ask in return, Charles," Barry said. "Otherwise it wouldn't be a friendship."

"Right," Charlemagne replied, uncrossing his arms. "Tell me, Barry. Do you remember that fusion reactor we drew up together?"

"The A-type? Of course!"

"With all the chaos, I forgot that it's gone into its initial testing. The results have been promising, and the future of clean energy lies before it."

"Really? When did it start its first test?"

"The preliminary test was in August and worked to a great success!" Charlemagne boasted. "They've been conducting additional tests almost every day to solve minor issues, but we should be able to reveal our work to the public by next spring if all goes well!"

"So, you're telling me that this fusion reactor was turned on in August, and had been turned on almost every day in the last couple of weeks?" Barry questioned, looking to Charlemagne.

The two looked at each other.

"Tell me, Charles. Does Cabernet Laboratories still close on the weekends?"

"No," Charlemagne replied in denial. "Not the reactor… it can't be source of all this. It's designed to be environmentally-friendly!"

"I don't think this is a by-product issue," Barry replied, leaning back in his chair. "Instead, this might be an issue in the start-up process, remember?"

"Even then, the entire fusion reaction is in a sealed chamber. Any emission of any sort of radiation is impossible!"

"I wouldn't say impossible," Barry remarked to him.

Charlemagne didn't reply as he scratched his head with a worried look.

"I'll have to see to it that the fusion reactor stops testing immediately, and if we don't see any uprisings on Monday, then we'll have our answer," Charlemagne remarked, grabbing his coat from the wall. "Until then, maintain that satellite over the county and let me know if that energy signature shows itself elsewhere."

"Sure thing," Barry replied as Charlemagne walked to the exit. "Keep me updated."

"I will."

Charlemagne left the observatory and walked down the steps to get to his car. He took out his phone and prepared to make some phone calls.

Act 5, Scene 3

Charlemagne sped along the freeway as he made his way to Cabernet Laboratories. His stomach turned as he saw the police cars parked along the curb of the front entrance with the boards removed from the front entrance. Charlemagne parked behind the police cars and got out to enter the foyer of the building.

"What's all this now?" Charlemagne complained, looking over to police with some security officers.

"Mr. Cabernet," Richard Huxley said, walking over to him from across the lobby. "There's been a terrible incident, Mr. Cabernet."

The young Chief Executive Officer of Cabernet Industries walked over to Charlemagne. He was a tall man in a fine pressed black suit. He had light brown hair like his son and blue eyes. He was carrying a briefcase in one hand.

"Please, Richard, 'Charles,'" he corrected. "What sort of incident?"

"A heist by the Medici family," Huxley said, bringing Charlemagne to security and police. "The oncoming security day shift had come to relieve the night shift only to find that they had all been killed at the hands of those thieves."

"No," Charlemagne replied, his head spinning.

"CCTV footage appears to show them stealing the fusion reactor from the restricted level, making their way out with most if not all of it."

"That's… that's not possible."

"Charles?" Richard questioned.

"I… I need to have a sit down," Charlemagne said, knees shaking.

Charlemagne fell onto a couch and brought his hand to his head. Richard walked over to him.

"I- I was just speaking with the Medici clan last night," Charlemagne said to him in a quiet voice. "How could they do this to me? How could they steal it?"

"You spoke with Giovanni?" Richard asked.

"No, Giovanni is dead. I spoke with Dino Medici," Charlemagne corrected. "I went to… to pay my sympathies over the deaths of him and Bianca, and it seemed as though all was fine between us. Do- do they blame me for their deaths?"

"Well, regardless, this has happened, Charles. I'll do what I can from my end and get into contact with the right people to take care of this."

"I- I don't believe you!" Charlemagne remarked to him. "Nobody was supposed to know about its existence except for a select few!"

"Please, Charles. Don't get mad," Richard reasoned with him.

"No, no, no!" Charlemagne said, standing up and pushing past Huxley. "I'm *going* mad…"

Charlemagne rushed over to the doors going deeper into the labs.

"You there!" Charlemagne shouted, pointing at a security guard. "Come with me!"

"Yes, sir," the security officer replied.

Charlemagne was let into the labs and brought to the service elevator. Huxley followed and the three came to the restricted sublevel where instead of turning left to go to the laboratory where the ghost was being held, they turned right to come to the end of the opposite-side where doors led into the fusion reactor chamber. The security officer tapped his card into the first door, leading them into a vestibule. The door on the other side was open with each door on the floor with black stains. Charlemagne walked over the doors and came to the metal catwalk around the large chamber where the fusion reactor was being kept.

The room was large and round. In the middle was where the reactor was formerly kept. Charlemagne put both arms on the railing as he looked around the room.

"With all due respect, Charles," Richard said. "You designed the reactor to be transportable… so the only real question is how Medici came to know that it existed, which comes down to a security breach. I assure you that we will get to the bottom of this."

"The issue is beyond that," Charlemagne remarked. "Just moments ago, I learned that the reactor was the source of all the recent spiritual uprisings… that reactor is not only the gateway towards clean energy, but also a weapon that could have disastrous consequences in the wrong hands."

"I'll make that clear to the investigators," Richard replied.

"No! The police cannot know that the reactor is the cause of the spiritual disturbances! Chief Phillips will use that against us and this could get raised to a matter of national concern."

"Okay, Charles, then what do I tell them?"

Charlemagne paused for a moment as he looked around the room. He then straightened up and turned.

"What does… What does the CCTV footage show?" Charlemagne asked, looking over to the security officer.

"I've only seen the footage once, but it appears to clearly show members of the Medici gang breaching the front doors before making their way towards the security office. They ambushed the team and took their proxy cards, letting them use the elevators. They then went down here and breached the doors. From there, we can see them rolling the device out and taking it upstairs."

"Right. Richard, ensure that police get the footage and that they are made aware that the fusion reactor poses no serious risks – that no radioactive material was taken and that all that was stolen was a prototype with no practical use."

"Yes, Charles."

The sound of an alarm could be heard from the corridor behind them. The security officer accompanying them looked at his pager.

"What now?" Charlemagne complained.

"I'm receiving a breach alarm at the Vault," the officer replied. "Two copies, breach alarm," he repeated into his radio.

"Take me there," Charlemagne requested.

Charlemagne left the chamber with the officer and the two went back to the service elevator to go down to the next sublevel. The elevator travelled downwards, shaking in the middle of its travel, causing the light to flicker and Charlemagne to grab the handle to hold on. The tremor lasted less than a couple of seconds before the elevator continued as normal. The two reached the second sublevel, which broke into three wide corridors. The second sublevel – the deepest level of the laboratories was set up in a grid-like manner. It contained pipes and electrical wires at the upper corners, overtop of a grate that ran slightly below the ceiling. Charlemagne and the officer went forward to travel past two intersections before reaching a set of thick blast doors that were halfway open.

"Oh, no, no, no," Charlemagne complained as he ran towards the doors.

Charlemagne entered the vault and looked around at the shelves of the large rectangular room. Plasma containers could be seen on the floor, open and empty. He picked one up and looked at before tossing it on the floor.

"Mr. Cabernet!" the security officer remarked from outside.

Charlemagne exited the room and went to him. He stood by a panel near the doors. Ectoplasm oozed out of the panel.

"No, not now... Will this nightmare never end?" Charlemagne cursed as he looked around.

A cold wind brushed against him next. Charlemagne looked around frantically as if he was looking for someone that had just passed by.

"Did you feel that?"

"No, sir," the officer replied. "Feel what?"

"Nevermind," Charlemagne said. "Stay here."

Charlemagne began to walk forward, looking around before he arrived at another intersection. He felt the wind again. He turned right and started to make his way to the next intersection before a brute wind hit him in the back, sending him onto the floor.

"The pain we feel is vain, and that is a pain that no one should suffer from," the feminine voice said. "He will make countless suffer the same vain pain."

"Who are you?" Charlemagne questioned from the ground. "Where do I find him?"

"You know who I am," the voice said as though distant.

"Mr. Cabernet!" Richard said, rushing over to Charles to help him.

"What happened?"

"I- I just had a bad fall is all," Charlemagne explained, standing up. "Thank you."

"I'll see to it that this breach is investigated," Richard said to him.

"Nevermind that," Charlemagne said. "All that was lost were specimens that I was going to release anyways... The true focus at the moment should be the return of the fusion reactor."

Act 5, Scene 4

Charlemagne spent the rest of the day dealing with the aftermath of the heist. He spoke with police investigators, recommending that Detective Hudson take the case due to his good relations with him. He then worked with Huxley to contain the situation at a business-level. By midday, Charlemagne went to the hospital to visit Dr. Lambert, who was still unconscious. Various other scientists who were injured had been able to return home, except for a few who Charlemagne also visited and spent time with.

In the evening, Charlemagne returned home to have dinner with the kids before setting to his study to make phone calls, one of which was to Barry to update each other on the current situation. At around midnight, Charlemagne retired to bed for the night.

The next morning, Charlemagne drove the kids to school and then went to the offices to report the situation at Cabernet Laboratories to the board. Charlemagne spent much of his time in his office space before driving the kids home and spending the evening in his study. No update for the missing fusion reactor came from the police. No notifications came at 1500 hours for pending cases. At 1700 hours, Charlemagne phoned Barry to report to confirm to him that the fusion reactor was the cause of all the uprisings. After this phone call, Charlemagne sat in his desk for several minutes before receiving a phone call himself.

"Charlemagne de la Cabernet speaking," Charlemagne said.

"Hello, Charles, this is Chief Phillips," a firm voice said. "If you're not busy at the moment, we would like you to come to the police station as soon as possible."

"I'll be there at once…"

"I require that you come with your ghost hunting gear, if you could."

"Copy that," Charlemagne replied.

The police chief hung up on him. Charlemagne set the phone down and stood up. He took a deep breath and put on a mild smile as he left the room. He went to the garage and went down the elevator to walk to his truck. There, he had left his things from last Friday. Charlemagne put on his jumpsuit and ensured all his items were in check before entering the truck to drive out. Sunset had passed, and it was now dark outside with clouds in the sky, but no rain.

Charlemagne sped along the road to come to downtown Allabrese just as he had in August when he wanted information on the first spiritual disturbance. He parked on the curb and got out of the truck. He went to the rear and got the beam cannon out. He loaded it with a plasma capsule and then equipped himself with his belt, stocked with all sorts of traps and gadgets.

"Let's hope this is the end of it all," Charlemagne told himself as he picked up his cannon and turned to face the station.

With those words, Charlemagne took his first steps forward and began to walk towards the front entrance of the police station. Through the glass door he noticed about a dozen police officers awaiting him. Charlemagne entered the main foyer and looked at all of them as they looked at him. Charlemagne held a smile towards them, looking around for Chief Phillips.

"Hello," Charlemagne greeted. "I'm here for Chief Phillips."

Once of the officers – one without much equipment and no vest took a radio from their belt and brought it to his mouth.

"Sir, he's here," the officer said.

"Copy, I'll be right down," the voice of Chief Phillips said.

Charlemagne's smile slowly faded as all the police officers began to intimidate him. Lightning flashed through the windows before the main doors opened and Chief Phillips exited with two armored police officers carrying automatic rifles.

"Chief Phillips," Charlemagne greeted.

"Hello Charles," the Chief replied. "Did you bring everything?"

"Certainly," Charlemagne remarked. "What seems to be the problem?"

The Chief sighed and looked at Charlemagne.

"You," the Chief replied. "I warned you, Charles, to not meddle in police affairs and unfortunately, you're under arrest for obstruction of justice."

The armored police officers pointed their weapons at Charlemagne.

"Drop your items," they said.

"What?!" Charlemagne questioned, dropping the cannon.

"Hands behind your back."

A police officer stepped forward to handcuff Charlemagne as he looked at Chief Phillips with a look of betrayal.

"We received an anonymous tip that you were at the Medici Estate and contaminated the crime scene. Not only did you contaminate possible fingerprints leading to the arrest of the murderer of Giovanni and Bianca Medici, but you also removed the corpse of Giovanni Medici, making you a prime suspect in their murder."

"What on Earth? I didn't move his corpse?!"

"You're making a serious mistake," Charlemagne reasoned. "Please, Phillips. Be understandable."

"Take him away," Phillips said, walking away. "Have all his belongings locked up and frisk him."

"You are going to regret this!" Charlemagne said, stepping forward. "The spirits are going to get worse! You need me!"

"Stop moving!" a police officer threatened.

“Come back here!” Charlemagne shouted at him. “Come and speak to me like a man!”

“Stun him,” another officer said as Charlemagne stepped forward again.

“Huh?” Charlemagne questioned before being jabbed in the side with an electrified baton.

Charlemagne fell to his knees and shouted in pain. The officer jabbed him again, causing him to fall to his side before blacking out.

Act 6, Scene 1

Diana leered at Tristan as he danced with Vivian Huxley on the dance floor in the middle of the gym.

"Go easy on 'em," Moira recommended, cutting Diana's concentration in reference to the brutal manner she was crushing her peanuts.

Shreds of peanut shell were strewn across the high-table the two of them were sitting at. Diana looked at the violent mess she had made and started to clean it up.

"Sorry, I didn't realize what I was doing," Diana nervously laughed as a flash of lightning filled the gym once more.

"What are we doing here again? Moira questioned as thunder boomed in the background. "I don't see how this is better than playing video games at my place."

"My guardian disappeared on me, and I was practically forced to come here or be alone at my place," Diana explained.

"Your guardian is missing?" Moira questioned, taking out her phone. "Here, watch me hack his phone to get his location. What's his number?"

Diana told her the number before she looked back over to Tristan.

"Alright, let's see where Mr. Cabernet is," Moira said, looking into her own phone. "Hm, according to this, he's at the police department. You see, he's fine."

Diana gently took her phone from her hands and looked at the map where it showed the location of Charlemagne's cellphone.

"What's he doing there?" Diana questioned, looking around the room as another flash of lightning lit the room.

"Who knows," Moira replied, taking her phone back.

"God, this party is *so* lame," Diana whined, tilting her head back.

"Don't you think I know that?" Moira laughed as Diana got out of her chair.

Moira followed her out of the gym and into the quiet hallway.

"I finished the book you lent me," Diana said as the two of them walked together. "I thought it was alright."

"Alright?"

"Well, I mean, I only prefer horror genre during October to amp me up for Halloween, so what you recommended me was a bit of a letdown."

"Psh, how uncultured of you," Moira replied.

"Uncultured? You're the one that only reads mystery novels. I'm the one that enjoys the classics," Diana grinned, looking at her friend with a smile.

Moira was dressed in light blue jeans, a yellow top and she was wearing her father's blue policeman rain jacket with the word, 'POLICE' on the back in reflective white letters, and the insignia of the county police on the shoulders.

The two of them looked at each other before turning their gaze down the hallway as they heard the sudden shatter of glass in the distance.

"What the hell?" Diana wondered.

Moira started to walk towards the noise to investigate as it was too dark to make out what was going on. Diana realized just what was going on as the two got closer and she noticed a hand reaching in through the glass.

"Is that… Mr. Whitmore?" Diana questioned. "Moira…"

The two of them made it in front of the school office where they looked at the hand trying to open the school door. The two simply stood there until the figure managed to turn the knob and push the door open.

"Jesus, aren't cigarettes supposed to make you calm? He looks pissed," Moira said.

"Maybe when he went out for his smoke break, he realized he was all out. That would make me pissed."

Mr. Whitmore seemed to be dressed for Halloween in his cheap brown suit. His grey hair was messy and long, and he was unshaven. He looked like a vagrant.

"Sir… are you alright?" Moira asked.

The teacher didn't reply.

"Maybe we shouldn't talk to him," Diana said to Moira, nudging her. "He doesn't look alright and I don't want to get into trouble right now."

Moira stepped forward and away from Diana in hopes of finding out if their teacher was okay. The man started to hover in the air as she made her way halfway towards him before he showed his face to show his mortifying face.

"Okay… that's not normal," Diana reacted, taking a single step forward towards Moira.

The man launched itself forward and grabbed Moira before Diana got the chance to take another step. It bashed her against the floor, stopped and stood up where she was to make a terrible screeching sound at Diana.

"Get off of her!" Diana yelled as the being edged forward, moving her own feet to launch herself forward in a sprint.

Moira scrambled for her phone on the ground, grabbed it and started to dial for Charlemagne's paranormal investigation hotline.

The man rushed towards Diana as she ran towards him, tackling him onto the ground before she started to punch him in the face. He hissed and screamed as she punched the man, causing a green slobber to come out of his face alongside blood. Diana hesitated another punch as she found her fist covered in the goop. The being pushed Diana off and caused her to fall onto the ground.

"Diana!" Moira yelled, rushing over to her and grabbing her by the arms to help her up.

"M-maybe we should go," Diana suggested as she looked the possessed man rise from the ground and float over the floor.

"Crap… maybe you're right," Moira reacted, turning her head to look at the spirit.

The two of them ran off and quickly made their way back into the rear hallway and down the left hall towards the cafeteria. The ghost landed in the corner and crashed into the wall. Moira and Diana turned around their corner and ran down the corridor outside of the cafeteria, going into the last classroom at the end of the hall. Diana quickly closed the door behind them and slid down against the door to hide with Moira.

"What the hell is going on?" Moira questioned in a hushed voice. "I swear that was Mr. Whitmore, but he was acting all… weird and ghost-like."

"Yeah, I'm not too sure what's going on either."

"Well, I phoned your old man either way," Moira added.

"Then let's hope that Charles gets his ass over here, stat," Diana said.

Diana paused for a moment to catch her breath. She looked around the classroom and then over to her friend.

"You know, I'm really glad you're seeing the same crap I am. Otherwise I'd swear I was going crazy or something," Diana said to her.

"Oh, of course," Moira smiled. "I still wouldn't rule out that this is all a dream."

Moira and Diana stood up to peak out the window.

“I think it’s gone,” Moira said.

“Moira…” Diana anxiously warned.

“Oh, don’t be such a baby,” Moira replied, opening the door and stepping out. “It’s gone.”

Diana walked over to her and they began to make their way to the end of the hall and back down to make their way to join the crowd of other students. They made their way into the gym and began to go back to their table. Diana looked around for the ghost before switching around to look for Tristan instead. The two of them pushed through the crowd of people dancing to the tune of loud techno. A flash of lightning could be seen through the window-tops of the gym before the thunder followed.

“Diana,” Moira warned, stopping her tracks and launching her hand to her shoulder to stop her from walking forward.

Diana looked over to the possessed-man thrashing around at the neon bar. The being was behaving like a child, pushing drinks over the edge and throwing bowls of nuts everywhere. The man made its way to a couple standing at the edge of the bar only aggravate the male dressed as an eighties Hawaiian private investigator.

“Hey, what the hell?!” Tristan yelled, turning to the man.

The possessed-man glared at Tristan with its glowing eyes and frown. It raised its hand in a crazed fashion and began to twitch its fingers at him.

“Tristan!” Diana yelled at him.

“Diana?” Tristan reacted, turning to the crowd to look for Diana.

“He’s possessed, Tristan! That’s not Mr. Whitmore! It’s a ghost!” Diana shouted to him before running forward.

“What?” Tristan questioned, looking back at the figure before it tackled him onto the floor. “Get off me!”

“Get your hands off of him!” Diana shouted as she grabbed the ghost from behind to try and pull it off.

The ghost let go of Tristan and instead repositioned its arms around his neck to choke him. Diana continued to struggle with it as they tried to get the possessed-man under control.

“Diana, watch out!” Moira warned from behind.

Diana turned her gaze and over to Moira as she held a bat. She immediately ducked as she prepped to swing and hit the being in the head. The possessed-man let go of Tristan. Tristan turned to crawl away and stand up.

“What the hell is wrong with him?!” Vivian yelled.

The creature was bent over and started to vomit ectoplasm on the floor before leaning back and yelling profusely.

“What is going on?” a parent chaperone asked, moving over to the bar. “Oh my God!”

“Tristan, text Charles. Tell him we’ve got a serious emergency,” Diana yelled to him.

“Yeah… good idea,” Tristan agreed, taking his phone out.

“Okay, everybody out!” the chaperone yelled. “Someone call the police!”

“I’m calling the police!” Tristan lied, dialing Charlemagne.

The possessed-man threw a ball of ectoplasm at the chaperone as everybody yelled and evacuated the gym and went into the hall. Diana took a step back with Moira as she glanced over to Tristan, trying to contact Charlemagne. The chaperone touched the gunk that splashed him before yelling and leaving the gym.

Tristan looked over to Diana as he put his phone away. He then began to look around for Vivian. The being threw another ball of ectoplasm over to Diana as it continued to yell in anguish. Diana dodged out of the way and grabbed Moira as it started to fly towards them. The two of them ran out of the gym, but it stopped going after them as a martini glass hit it on the side.

"Hey, ugly!" Tristan yelled. "Weren't you going after me just now? Huh? Come and get me instead of them!"

Tristan threw another glass, hitting it on the face before running off. The being yelled and went after him, almost swooping for him, but Tristan ducked. Diana and Moira entered the hallway and met with the rest of the crowd at the front entrance. They had stopped just before the door.

"Oh my God!" Vivian shrieked. "There's more of them out there!"

"Everybody, please remain calm," a different chaperone requested.

"Into this classroom! We'll be safe in here!" the other chaperone said.

Diana and Moira watched as the crowd started to enter the classroom before Diana turned to see Tristan enter the hallway from the rear corridor.

"Tristan!" Diana shouted in relief.

"Where's the ghost?" Moira questioned.

The possessed-man gave a loud yell from the end of the hall just as Moira finished her question.

"Still need an answer?" Tristan replied, turning around and running towards them.

"Where's Charlemagne?" Diana questioned. "He should be here by now!"

"Maybe he's a little busy at the moment," Tristan remarked, joining the others.

"With the swarm of ghosts outside? Yeah, maybe just a little busy…" Moira groaned.

"What can we do then?" Diana asked as the ghost began to throw ectoplasm towards them.

The possessed-man began to charge towards them again with two balls of ectoplasm in its hands.

"We run!" Tristan remarked, rushing back into the hall towards the gym with them.

The trio made their way into the gym. Diana tripped along some wires to the DJ booth, causing her to crash into the floor. Tristan stopped and turned around to look at her. He then immediately went after her. The being threw balls of ectoplasm towards them before preparing to grab Diana. Tristan helped Diana up and the two of them ran off and crouched under a high-table. The being knocked into the table, causing it to tip over. It flew past them and started to make its way towards Moira. Diana noticed and started to sprint towards the creature as it made its pass towards her. She grabbed the creature by the waist. The being screamed and shrieked, flying around the gym as she maintained her grip.

Tristan looked at the ghost as it flew around, trying to get Diana to let go as it purposely crashed into walls of the gymnasium.

"Tristan!" Moira yelled. "What can we do?"

"I don't know," Tristan replied, shrugging.

"You're Charlemagne's protégé!" Diana shouted. "Think of anything!"

Tristan paused for a moment as he looked at the being with fear. He then looked around the room, towards the bar and then the stage before looking to the DJ booth and electrical wires. Diana crashed the creature into the catwalk over the stage, falling onto the platform with the being.

"Moira, get out of here!" Tristan yelled to her. "I've got an idea, but I need the thing to target me. Close the doors of the gym and get out! Rendezvous with Charlemagne at the main entrance! I've got this!"

"Sure thing," Moira replied, rushing out and closing the doors behind her.

Tristan picked up the bat on the floor and began to tap it on the floor to get the being's attention. He then grabbed another martini glass on the floor and threw it at the creature.

"Hey, over here!" Tristan yelled. "You forgot about me!"

The possessed shifted its view from Diana to Tristan after the martini glass hit it in the face. The creature hissed at him and launched itself from the platform to fly at him. Tristan ran off towards a trapdoor in the floorboards, opened it and started to climb down. Diana climbed down the catwalk and tackled the creature at the trapdoor. The thing fell onto the floor and began to wriggle around as Diana hugged it. She looked to the side as the last gym doors closed thanks to Moira before letting go of the creature and jumping down the trapdoor to join Tristan.

Diana looked around the many pipes in the dimly lit room before freaking out over the sudden hand around her mouth. She elbowed whoever was behind her in the stomach, causing him to let go and the two to look at each.

"Oh crap! Sorry," Diana apologized, looking at Tristan.

"It's okay," Tristan replied in a whisper, straightening himself up as he looked at Diana. "That thing is coming for us, so I'll be quick with what I've done. This place runs like a race circuit. It's time to prove yourself for the sprinter you brag to be. Let that thing see you before you start to run and let it chase you. I'm going to finish fixing some wires before switching on the power again. When it comes near, try and not get caught. I'll switch the power back on once you're safely through."

The being fell down the hatch and began to wriggle around on the floor.

"Good luck," Tristan said, patting Diana on the shoulder before disappearing into the darkness.

"Wait, Tristan!" she remarked before looking over to the creature. "Can you run that by me one more time?"

The creature stood up and began to tap its hands along the pipes.

"Just go!" Tristan shouted.

The possessed-man screamed at Diana, and she stepped back and started to run forward. She came around the first corner as Tristan began to fool around with some wires. Diana could barely see had it not been for the bit of moonlight seeping in through the small windows at the top of the walls. The man crashed head first into the pipes at the first corner. Diana continued forward, going down the narrow corridor and towards the next corner as the ghost charged towards her.

Tristan quickly tied the wires together and looked through the pipes to see Diana coming towards the third and fourth corners. He began to tighten the wires as best he could before going to the electrical switch in the nook near the workbench and other janitorial tools. Diana ran down the hall and began to see the trap laid by Tristan as she turned the fourth corner. The man screamed behind her, forcing her to keep going forward only to drop her body as she was about two meters from the wire to push her legs straightforward to slide underneath. Diana felt a split wire cut her along the cheek as she pushed through.

Tristan watched Diana crash with amazement before he switched the power on and ran over to help Diana up. The man crashed into the wires and began to twitch as it was electrocuted. Sparks flew around.

Diana got up and looked over at the being as it violently quivered with its arms spread along the wiring until the wire snapped over the pressure. Tristan took a step back as the man fell before them. The creature jittered gently on the floor. The ghost twitched before calming down in paralysis. Diana and

Tristan quickly rushed over to Mr. Whitmore passed out on the ground. Tristan felt for a pulse at his wrist before the two carried him into a storage closet, rushed out, and closed the door behind them. Diana found a chair and quickly put it at the door knob to prevent it from escaping afterwards. Tristan knelt down and put his hands on his knees while Diana leaned against the door in a pant.

"Nice job," Diana said to him as she caught her breath. "You really held your own back there."

"Yeah, ditto," Tristan replied, straightening up and looking over to her.

Diana slid down the door to rest her back against it while Tristan continued to gaze at her before joining her. Tristan began to smile for a second as he slid down and gave off a laugh. Diana looked over to him as he chuckled before she smiled at him. The two laughed with each other as they calmed down and relaxed.

Act 6, Scene 2

"I'm not supposed to be in here!" Charlemagne complained, moving back and forth in his cell. "Let me go!"

Charlemagne waited for the officer responsible for him to yell back at him to shut up, but not a single whisper came back. Charlemagne waited an extra second before breaking his routine and grabbing the bars of his cell to try and look down the corridor. He looked around and noticed that he was alone. He stepped back and sat down on the bench.

"Hello?" a feminine voice questioned in the distance.

"Hello?" Charlemagne replied, rushing back over to the bars.

Charlemagne looked down the corridor as he saw Sabrina Phillips enter the cell block. She was dressed in rain coat and black dress. She walked over to where Charlemagne was and looked to him. Her eyes were blue instead of their normal green.

"You're not Sabrina," Charlemagne remarked, looking to her as she walked over.

"It is happening," she replied. "The undead are rising in great numbers and running rampant in our beloved town."

"And here I am locked up," Charlemagne replied.

"Like the spirits you entrapped to keep like pets."

"I broke the law," Charlemagne objected.

"Justifiably so," Curtia affirmed, looking at him. "You don't have time to lose if you wish to stop him."

Curtia took a keycard from her pocket and passed it to Charlemagne.

"The constabulary is stretched thin and their pain has become the pain of the living," Curtia explained. "Get your items and go correct your error before it is too late."

"Where is the reactor? What pain? Tell me more," Charlemagne pleaded as he opened his cell door.

"The pain of being brought to the physical world once more..." Curtia explained to him. "How else is one to react to being whisked back here?"

Charlemagne opened the gate and looked around the corridor. He looked over to Sabrina, possessed with the spirit of her grandmother.

"Where are my things?" Charlemagne asked. "Where's the reactor and Nero?"

Sabrina's eyes changed back to their natural color. She fell over and collapsed onto the floor. Charlemagne knelt down to make she was okay.

"Sabrina?" Charlemagne questioned, shaking her.

"Huh?"

Sabrina woke up and pushed herself off from the ground.

"Charlemagne?" she asked. "What am I doing here? Where am I?"

"You're in the dungeon of your husband's citadel, my dear," Charlemagne explained. "Come on."

Charlemagne helped her onto her feet.

"What do you last remember?" he asked.

"I-I believe I was at home when I started to think of my mother... and then I got a phone call from Cole. He told me there was a serious emergency in the town, and then I started to worry... that's the last of what I remember."

"Is that all?"

"No. I also heard... a voice. Not a schizophrenic voice, but an inner voice like a conscience – my own voice, telling me that I needed to do something to help."

"Well, you just helped me out of my cell, so that's plenty of help. Come on, we need to talk to your husband. Perhaps you can also help by talking some sense into him..."

Charlemagne let go of Sabrina and started to lead them out of the cell block. At the end of the corridor was a door labeled 'Evidence Lockup.' Charlemagne brought the keycard to the proxy pad and the door opened. Inside was an assortment of items including Charlemagne's tools. He put together his things and made sure nothing was damaged. He then put on his belt and picked up the cannon to leave. Charlemagne also retrieved his cellphone, which he turned on to read all of the notifications he had received over the last hour.

"My God…" Charlemagne expressed, scrolling through them all.

Charlemagne put his phone away and began to leave with Sabrina. The two of them came to the elevator and tapped to go up. Charlemagne tapped the proxy card and then the doors closed. The elevator started to go up. Charlemagne looked to Sabrina. She had a worried look on her face and she was silent.

"You know," Charlemagne said. "You and your grandmother, Curtia, are quite similar."

Sabrina gave a small smile to Charlemagne.

"Both of you have kind hearts and innocent spirits," Charlemagne added. "She lives on in you. You know that, right?"

Sabrina looked at Charlemagne, but didn't reply. The elevator doors opened, and the two of them stepped out. The two of them heard metal clanking and the sound of glass shattering, causing them to hurry to Chief Phillips' office.

"Help me! Somebody, please!" Phillips yelled.

Charlemagne held the cannon tightly at its grip and burst through the door. There in the office, he found the chief being held hostage by a police officer with only the white of his eyes showing. He had a red glow to him and held a knife to the chief's neck.

"Stand back or this pig gets it!" the possessed-officer warned.

"Let him go!" Charlemagne demanded, pointing the cannon towards the being.

"Charles! Thank God!" Phillips cried. "Do something!"

"Don't even think about!" the ghost threatened. "Or I'll slice this pig!"

"Oh, please no! I have a family!" Phillips yelled.

"So did I!"

Charlemagne's eyes scanned the room. His eyes wandered from item to item before focusing on the rear of the computer. Specifically, on the device he inserted in August to hack into the chief's computer.

"Alright, I'll cooperate with you," Charlemagne said, lowering the cannon so that he held it with one hand.

"What?! What are you doing?!" Phillips questioned.

"Charles," Sabrina protested.

"Just let him go," Charlemagne said, gently lowering the cannon onto the floor.

"Here's how this is going to play," the spirit began to say. "I'm going to leave here with this little pig, but I want you two to step out of the way."

Charlemagne brought his hands together. He then started to bring his right hand up towards his watch as the ghost droned on, digging underneath his watch where there was a thin bracelet. Charlemagne slowly and carefully pressed a button on the bracelet.

The device on the chief's computer exploded, allowing Charlemagne to quickly grab the cannon again as the possessed-officer and chief were knocked back, and the grip of the spirit around the chief was broken. Charlemagne raised the cannon and aimed it at the officer before he fired. The beam knocked the officer back and against the wall.

The officer was knocked out, causing Charlemagne to look around and quickly bring his goggles down. A cold spot rose from the officer. Charlemagne fired at it and kept his weapon steady. The glass window behind the chief exploded as the spirit attempted to escape, but Charlemagne maintained his grip before the spirit was sucked into the capsule and the beam cut-off. He quickly removed the capsule and set it on the ground.

A flash of lightning lit the room. Charlemagne picked up the capsule and brought it over to the chief's desk.

"Is it done?" the chief asked.

"I warned you," Charlemagne said to the chief.

"You didn't warn me about anything!" the chief barked.

"Enough!" Sabrina yelled at them. "What is with you two?! You're always at each other's throats! Cole, what is with this prejudice towards Charlemagne? He's done nothing wrong against you!"

"Sabrina…" Cole replied. "He's a criminal! He's broken the law!"

"He just saved you," Sabrina countered. "Had he not, you'd be dead right now. This has nothing to do with the law or upholding the law. This is about your own selfishness and jealousy…. something of which isn't appropriate at the moment – you two need to learn to cooperate."

Phillips rolled his eyes.

"He tampered with police evidence, Sabrina! He's a prime suspect in an important murder case! It's more than my jurisdiction to pardon him – it's up to the province!"

"I didn't murder Giovanni," Charlemagne objected. "I didn't take his corpse either! He was murdered by Nero Medici."

"That's preposterous," Phillips objected. "Nero is dead."

"You were just attacked by a fellow officer possessed by the spirit of his criminal father… possibly due to this man's own devil and prejudice against the law that took his father from him," Charlemagne remarked, looking over to the unconscious police officer. "Is it so preposterous to believe that a vile crime lord came back from the dead, possessed his grandson and executed his own child? It's a murder case that would never be solved, and because of me, you now know the truth. Your ego outweighs your conviction to uphold your precious man-made laws. Your selfishness consumes you!"

"I could have handled it all on my own!" Phillips barked. "I don't need your help! I'm sending you back down there as soon as this is over!"

"Cole!" Sabrina shouted.

"If you believe you can end this uprising all on your own, then by all means, arrest me. I'm one man against a hundred more of these. You could barely handle yourself against this one. We both need each other if we're to end this crisis on both our hands. I need your help, and you need mine."

"Charlemagne is right, Cole," Sabrina said. "If you really cared about doing good, you would be working with Charles, not antagonizing him. Please… enough is enough."

Phillips scowled at him. Charlemagne let go of the capsule and brought his hand over to shake hands with Phillips. Phillips took his hand and the two shook.

"Alright, what can be done?" Phillips asked with an unhappy expression. "My boys are being overrun done there."

"I'm going to go after the source of all this chaos. I have a satellite over the county that can find out the source of all this. I need your men to take care of the situation downtown by neutralizing all of the possessed. A simple electrical shock should do the trick. Do you think your men can handle that?"

"Is that all?" Phillips wondered. "Is that all it takes?"

"It's enough to entrap the spirit in an unconscious body for the night," Charlemagne explained.

"Alright," Phillips replied. "We'll handle the situation out here. You put an end to the cause of all this though!"

"Will do."

Charlemagne took a step back and started to leave.

"And Charles," Phillips said, stopping him by the door. "Don't die out there."

Charlemagne nodded before he left.

Act 6, Scene 3

Charlemagne walked out of the Nattau Police Department building and gave a long look at the surrounding town. The sound of sirens and screams of people in the distance could be heard. Lightning lit up the sky and the moon peaked out from the clouds. A tormentous rain hit down with additional thunder crying out.

The pick-up truck was still parked along the curb. Charlemagne made his way over and got inside quickly so he could get out of the rain. He looked out of the glass and could see people roaming around, seeming lost. He took out his phone and called Barry.

"Barry," Charlemagne greeted.

"Charles, what's up?"

"I don't take it that you're watching the evening news, are you?" Charlemagne said, starting the truck.

"No, why?"

"All hell has broken loose down here, that's why," Charlemagne explained. "I need you to look to the satellite feed and tell me if you see that signature."

"Sure thing, Charles," Barry replied. "Sorry, I didn't realize what was going on."

"It's all right, friend," Charlemagne said, turning on the windshield wipers. "I've just been in cells for the past couple of hours."

The sky flashed as Charlemagne waited for Barry to give him an update.

"There it is!" Barry exclaimed. "I just saw it! A burst of that radiation just came from Allabrese Cemetery!"

"Of course," Charlemagne sighed. "What better place to sit the device than the place of the dead. Okay, Barry. I'm going to go and end this once and for all."

"I'll monitor the satellite from here in case the reactor moves or anything. They won't get away from us!"

"Roger that," Charlemagne replied, hanging up.

Charlemagne tossed his phone onto the dashboard before changing gears. He then pulled out and started to drive. He started to make a U-turn, braking immediately as a body hit the windshield.

"Good Lord!" Charlemagne shouted, raising up the parking brake.

Charlemagne immediately opened the door and looked to the man in a flannel shirt on the road.

"Are you okay?!" Charlemagne cried out.

The man began to laugh maniacally before rolling around on the wet road. Charlemagne shook his head and closed the door before driving off towards the cemetery.

"Bloody ghosts," Charlemagne cursed.

Charlemagne drove through town and made his way down the same road that went over the bridge only to turn and head north along the coastal road instead. He drove along and began to speed up before coming to the exit that went to the canyon where Allabrese Cemetery was.

At the entrance of the cemetery, Charlemagne noticed gunfire coming from the grounds. A small group of men in blue suits hiding behind tombstones were fighting against a small crowd at the base of the hill also in blue suits but hiding behind vintage black sedans. Charlemagne drove up and joined them, exiting his car to hide behind it.

In the group of individuals behind the cars, he saw Dino at the end. Charlemagne made his way towards him with his equipment.

"Charlemagne," the mobster said. "Nice of you to join us finally."

"What's going on?" Charlemagne asked, holding his weapon steady.

"We're being pinned down," Dino explained. "A couple days ago, Giovanni made an appearance at a meeting and announced himself as alive. Naturally, having seen the body and knowing what I knew, I was suspicious. Of course, it was really Nero and a couple hours ago, he took Arturo and the other boys out with him. I insisted I joined, Giovanni – I mean, Nero – refused. He attacked me. I called you. You didn't show, so I rallied what men I have to fight against those loyal to him, and now we're here."

A bright flash of light filled the sky. The Earth tremored.

"I'm sorry, I was held up at the police station. I should have suspected this when I heard that the corpse of Giovanni was missing and that Medici members were caught stealing from my labs. I've been too caught up in other things."

"No worries, Mr. Cabernet."

"Listen, I'm going to need your help," Charlemagne said to him. "I need to confront Nero and send him back to the hell he belongs in. He has the cause of all of this, and if I stop him, I can stop all of this."

"Mr. Cabernet... that's the most ridiculous thing I've heard, but sadly, I trust you right now. Please help us, help you."

"Exactly," Charlemagne replied. "You maintain your men at this defensive position to provide some covering fire. I'm going to breakthrough and drive towards the deeper cemetery to get to Nero. Does this sound okay with you?"

"Sure, we'll hold this line," Dino said.

"Excellent," Charlemagne said. "Wait for me to get back to my vehicle, and I'll sound the horn when I'm ready."

"Sure," Dino replied.

Charlemagne started to make his way back to his car.

"Hold the line!" Dino shouted to his men. "Prepare to provide covering fire!"

Charlemagne snuck back to his truck, ducking from the bullets flying overhead. He got into the driver seat and quickly turned the engine on to drive around and start to drive away before making a U-turn. He aimed the car towards the hill and gate. He then honked the horn. The mobsters at the base of the hill began to unleash a barrage of bullets towards those at the top. Charlemagne put his foot down onto the accelerator

The truck met the wet dirt of the hill and he started to make his way towards the concrete path going toward the gates. He ducked from the bullets that riddled the side of the truck. The shower of gunfire ended as he bashed through the gates and drove along the path, going into the depths of the graveyard.

The truck continued to speed along the path. Charlemagne sat up and looked out the windshield as he drove at an astonishing velocity. The wipers couldn't keep up with the rain. Another flash lit up in the sky from the fusion reactor which he saw in the distance. Charlemagne put his foot on the brakes and caught sight of a dark figure along the cliffs over the reactor. The figure shot bullets towards him before balls of ectoplasm hit the windshield to block his view. Charlemagne lost control of the vehicle and started to swerve. In a sudden instant, the truck crashed into a dead tree and came to a halt.

Charlemagne's body rested against the airbags. He quickly recovered and opened the doors to get out, taking his beam cannon with him.

“So,” a loud and old voice shouted from the top of the cliff, “if it isn’t Charlemagne de la Cabernet, the rich old prince of Allabrese.”

Charlemagne looked over to Nero as he shut the door to his car. He began to walk towards a set of steps going towards the reactor and caught a better sight of the mobster. The spirit of Nero Medici possessed his former corpse, rotted and purple in a dirty black suit with a red tie. He had both eyes intact and a black fedora with a white ribbon. He held a Thompson machine gun in one hand, pointed upwards as he pointed with the other hand at Cabernet. He sat atop of a cliff overlooking the main cemetery, which was built in the center of a canyon. Steps on either side of the reactor led up to the perch where the mobster was, which in itself was in front of another perch. There were about three layers to the cliffs of the canyon.

“I knew you’d be trouble from the moment I saw you at the manor house!” Nero shouted. “I contemplated killing you and taking over you instead, but the appeal of the young boy, to be young again, was much more inviting.”

Charlemagne’s eyes moved down to the fusion reactor, which was an intricate design. The metal of the reactor was a dark grey. Inside of the reactor was an artificial star, which could be seen through the center of the donut-shaped magnets that covered each of the six sides. In the space between each donut were conduits with lasers pointed inwards. The star itself was trapped inside of a glass sphere, which was exposed only at the top due to a missing top that could be seen half-buried in the mud nearby. Inside of the sphere, the artificial star was surrounded by a metal cage that looped around. The fusion reactor was hooked up to various gasoline-powered generators all around.

The artificial star was pulsating and struggling to maintain its size. Nearby the reactor were the Medici boys, Arturo, Bruno, and Mercutio, tied to a pole. Near the boys was Nero's grave, dug up with the corpse of Giovanni on the ground next to it.

"I heard a lot about you from the other spirits," Nero proclaimed. "Even amongst the dead, you are renowned. I expect the same fame when I crush you and have the Medici clan rise once more over those that destroyed us!"

Charlemagne ducked out of the way and hid behind a tombstone as the gangster began to fire towards him. He remained there for a moment, hands on the beam cannon and breathing steadily. The gangster stopped firing to reload, giving Charlemagne opportunity to move out and strike. Charlemagne opened fire with the beam cannon, striking the rocks of the cliff as Nero jumped out of the way.

The artificial star flashed as it died out and was reborn again into a large sphere of plasma. Charlemagne was momentarily blinded, causing him to fall to the ground and scramble for cover. He heard the laughter of Nero. The mobster began to fire again. Charlemagne shouted in pain as he felt his arm cut by the passing of a bullet.

Charlemagne blinked several times until he could see once more. He took a brief break before picking up his cannon and waiting for the gangster to reload again. He turned to watch Nero fly from the perch he was at and step down to start to make his way towards Charlemagne. Charlemagne prepared a trap from his belt, set it down where he was and then got up to run back the truck. Charlemagne hid behind the truck and knelt down with the cannon aimed. The trap detonated as Nero passed, giving Charlemagne opportunity to shoot at him.

The beam cannon hit the corpse of the gangster and caused him to be knocked back. Charlemagne immediately switched on his thermal vision as he noticed the corpse become inanimate. The cold spot that was Nero moved from where it was and ran off. Charlemagne pushed forward and saw it run to the corpse of Giovanni, animating it. The corpse stood up and picked up a pistol nearby. Charlemagne ducked behind another tombstone, one closer to the reactor as the ghost started to fire.

"You can't get rid of me!" Nero shouted.

Charlemagne remained in cover. He heard the ghost stop firing and peaked around the corner. The possessed-corpse of Giovanni jumped back onto the cliff and was making its way around to flank Charlemagne. Charlemagne ran across the pathway and hid behind a large tomb. The mobster started to open fire at him. Charlemagne prepared his cannon to fire as soon as he heard the click of wasted ammunition.

The beam cannon fired once the mob boss was out. Nero jumped out of the way and came to the ground. He ran around the reactor and arrived at Arturo, taking a knife from his blazer to release the boy. Charlemagne fired at Giovanni, striking him in the chest and causing him to fly backwards.

"No!" Charlemagne complained, realizing what he had just done.

The spirit of Nero flew up and into Arturo, sending the boy onto the ground.

"Arturo!" Charlemagne shouted, running towards him.

The boy seized on the ground, squirming and twitching as the ghost wrestled with the young boy's soul. Charlemagne arrived at the boy and knelt down beside him. He tried to control him, looking into the white of his eyes that rolled back.

"Arturo," Charlemagne said. "You mustn't give in. You must fight back!"

Arturo hit Charlemagne in the face before throwing balls of ectoplasm at him.

"The boy is no more," Nero said. "Innocent Arturo couldn't resist learning more about his triumphant grandfather – a man greater than his own father – a man that led the Medici clan during the dark times, ensuring our survival instead of one too afraid to fight – one lost in the underground between two ideas. What a useless and indecisive bastard!"

"You destroyed the Medici namesake," Charlemagne objected. "Your criminal antics destroyed the prestige the Medici name used to have and reduced yourselves to a corrupt mafia hiding behind waste management and construction. What a fall from the banking empire you once owned… built by your ancestors… reduced into nothing by you!"

"You know nothing!" Nero remarked, firing more ectoplasm towards him. "Our empire was stolen from us!"

Nero jumped up onto the cliff and volleyed ectoplasm from there. Charlemagne hid behind the reactor. He started to crouch his way around the left-side and made his way to the edge of the cliff. Nero jumped down to where Charlemagne formerly was.

"Where did you go?" Nero complained.

Charlemagne snuck behind the possessed-boy and grabbed him.

"Let go!"

"Arturo!" Charlemagne cried out. "I know you're still there! You need to fight him! Do not let him deceive you! You need to fight him and know that you can be better than him!"

"Shut up!"

"You need to fight him, Arturo! You can't let him consume you! He's nothing! His greed bankrupted your family – you cannot let him manipulate you to believe otherwise!"

"No…!" Arturo yelled. "Get out!"

The fusion reactor flashed and Arturo became unconscious in Charlemagne's arms. Charlemagne watched as the spirit ran off and went towards his own corpse. The corpse of Nero Medici became re-animated again.

"Are you okay?" Charlemagne asked Arturo.

"What happened?" he asked.

"Watch out!" Charlemagne cried out, pushing the boy out of the way before he jumped out and into cover behind a tombstone.

The mobster began to fire again before jumping forward. Arturo looked at his grandfather as Nero looked at Charlemagne. He brought up his Thompson and prepared to fire at him, but Arturo quickly tackled him onto the ground.

"No more!" Arturo shouted, thrashing at his grandfather.

Charlemagne ran for his beam cannon and grabbed it behind the two as they wrestled. Nero threw his grandson off and ran to grab him as Charlemagne prepared to fire. The ghost jumped up onto the cliff with his grandson, causing Charlemagne to rush up the steps to meet them up there. He came to top of the cliff and faced Nero as he held his grandson hostage in a chokehold.

"Face it, there's no way you win," Nero said. "You hit me with that thing, and I come back in another body. I'm immortal."

"I'll wipe you out of existence!" Charlemagne shouted.

Nero laughed as Arturo thrashed in his grip. The boy finally managed to get loose, elbowing his grandfather before attempting to run off. The elbowing did little, but Nero did attempt to grab him again, allowing Charlemagne to bring up the cannon and fire at him. He missed, hitting the ground instead, causing the rock to crumble and the two of them to fall a level.

Charlemagne rushed over to get to the edge of the cliff, but as he ran, he was jumped by the cold spirit of Nero, sending him back. Charlemagne quickly scrambled for his cannon and fired at the being, catching it in a grip of the plasma beam. Nero resisted the force that sucked him in. Charlemagne began to lose his grip. The two were in a struggle against one another, and the beam cannon started to overheat.

In a quick decision, Charlemagne let go of the spirit and sent it flying backwards. The force of Nero pulling away from the beam gave a counter force that caused Charlemagne to jump forward and come to the next level. There, Charlemagne again launched the beam towards the spirit as it ran to the corpse of Nero. He fired the cannon and missed for the ground. Nero pushed himself off from the ground. Charlemagne tossed the beam cannon aside and ran for him before he grabbed the submachine gun, tackling him onto the ground.

Nero knocked Charlemagne back, but Charlemagne quickly recovered to pull him away and to the other side. Charlemagne kicked the ghoul and he started to run off and head towards the plasma cannon, throwing it towards Charlemagne. Charlemagne ducked and ran to tackle the spirit onto the ground again before picking him up and bringing him to the edge of the cliff with the fusion reactor below.

"No!" Nero yelled. "Stop!"

The corpse of Nero caught fire from the proximity to the artificial star.

"I know things that you'd like to know, Mr. Cabernet," the spirit said. "Don't you want to know who it was that betrayed you? Who told me about this contraption? Who our client is?"

"Speak then!" Charlemagne barked. "Who is the mole?! Who are you working for?!"

"L-let me go!" Nero yelled as his hat fell off and into the reactor.

Charlemagne looked at the man with hateful eyes. The fire on the jacket of the man spread and singed Charlemagne's hand, causing him to let go. The ghoul fell over and into the reactor, and when his body met with the artificial star, Charlemagne quickly looked away as the star let out a burst of energy from the reactor chamber that caused all of the gasoline generators to explode around the cemetery. Charlemagne looked down to the reactor shut down and saw there to be nothing left of Nero Medici in existence.

Arturo rushed over to look down with him. The two of them then made their way downhill to free the others.

"Is everybody okay?" Charlemagne asked.

The boys all nodded. Charlemagne looked at all of them with relief before looking at what they were looking at: either the grave of Nero Medici, the tombstone of which had been smashed in half due to a nearby generator that exploded, or the corpse of their father which stood halfway between them and the grave.

Charlemagne brought his hands around the boys and decided to lead them away from both, and towards the truck where he expected the others to arrive soon. A convoy of vehicles soon turned up along the paved road leading to the truck. The frontmost car was occupied by Dino, who promptly got out to wave towards them.

"Arturo! Bruno! Mercutio!" the man yelled, running towards them and embracing all three. "I'm glad all three of you are alright. Thank you, Mr. Cabernet, but where's Nero?"

"He's gone," Charlemagne said.

"He escaped?"

"No, he's gone as in, he doesn't exist anymore. There is no remnant of that foul man in either body or soul."

"Good riddance," Dino said. "Come on, boys. Let's get you out of this rain."

Other mobsters moved out of the vehicle and began to move towards the grave and Giovanni's corpse with a duffel bag while Dino led the boys away from the scene. Charlemagne began to go up the steps to collect his things when Dino turned around after letting the boys into the car.

"Mr. Cabernet, wait," Dino said, walking over to him.

Charlemagne turned to face him.

"On behalf of the Medici name, I am deeply sorry for the plot and conspiracy against you and your loved ones. Rest assured, you and your loved ones are under our special protection from now on from all that threatens them. We are in your debt, Mr. Cabernet."

"I appreciate the gesture," Charlemagne replied, looking to him. "For the sake of the Medici name, all I wish however is that the name can be restored to its former glory. See to it that the Medici family quits this vile life of crime and restore its honor and nobility."

Dino and Charlemagne looked to each other. Dino simply nodded before turning around. Charlemagne looked to Arturo who was looking to him from the car and listening. Charlemagne nodded to him as a gesture of farewell before turning around.

"Can I offer you a ride back to town, Mr. Cabernet," Dino offered.

"No need!" Charlemagne replied, not turning around. "I have business here I need to finish up – I've got to get this bloody machine back to the labs before anyone comes for it."

"Understood, Mr. Cabernet!" Dino yelled. "Farewell."

Dino shouted to some of his men in Italian as Charlemagne went to find his beam cannon. He picked it up and carried it back to the truck, sitting in the passenger seat as he took out his phone to see several missed notifications from the hotline as well as a missed call from both Barry Lambert, Richard Huxley, and Judith Lambert. Charlemagne's eyebrows raised as he read Judith Lambert's name. He quickly opened his voicemail and went through his messages.

"Charles, it's me, Judith. I'm listening to the radio about the awful things happening in downtown. I hope you're alright. Please, be careful and know that we're counting on you."

"Charles," Richard said. "I got word from your attorney about your situation at the police department. Don't you worry, my friend. I'll make sure you get out as soon as possible!"

"Hey, Charles the Great," Barry said. "I hope you're doing alright. I've stopped picking up readings from the fusion reactor, which either tells me that you did it, or we're all doomed and you failed. Give me a shout when you can."

Charlemagne took his phone away from his ear and looked to the message from Tristan, asking him to come to the school before looking at the next which told him to disregard the former message and telling him that he and Diana took care of everything and are fine. Charlemagne responded with a quick message stating that he was on his way to pick them up. Afterwards, Charlemagne got out of the truck as the rest of the Medici family members were leaving in their cars. He began to call someone on the phone as he walked over to look to the reactor.

"Hello Richard," Charlemagne said, "quite an evening we're all having, isn't it? I need you to do me a quick favor and have police come to Allabrese Cemetery to secure the fusion reactor. I then need you to send a private security team to relieve them and pick up the reactor.

"Sure thing, Charles," Richard replied. "Are you okay? Is everything good?"

"Yes, friend. All is good. I've got lots to discuss with you in the morning. Until then, try and take it easy."

"Of course, Charles."

Charlemagne hung up and then looked past the reactor. He walked over to what was a large tombstone against the cliff, with the name of his hero, 'Derby de la Cabernet' engraved in memory. Charlemagne looked at the grave as he waited for several minutes before a police team was dispatched to guard the reactor, relieving him to go and pick up the kids. He continued to look at the grave however until he felt the weight of a hand on his shoulder. Charlemagne turned around to see who was behind him, but there was no one. He looked around and then stared into the glass of the reactor, seeing the reflection of someone similar in appearance to him before he shook his head to see himself in the mirror. He paused for a moment before moving to leave.

Charlemagne got into the pickup truck where he pushed the windshield glass out so that he could see. He then started the truck and backed up to drive out of the cemetery, around the police cruisers. Once he was on the road, he dialed Barry on speaker phone and talked his friend as he drove back to town.

Act 6, Scene 4

Diana and Tristan walked down the main hall together, casually conversing as they left with everybody else. A large sum of parents were parked outside, reuniting with their children. The rain had stopped, but there was now a chill in the air.

"I guess it's all over," Diana exhaled, looking around.

"Yeah, thank God it's all over," Tristan replied as they stood at the top of the steps.

"Tristan!" a high pitched voice squealed from behind them. "My hero!"

The two of them turned around as Vivian Huxley made her way over to embrace Tristan. He jumped as her arms wrapped around him.

"You saved us, didn't you?!" she proclaimed before hiving a smooch on the lips.

Tristan's cheeks flushed red and Diana's green. Vivian soon parted and let go of him before waving goodbye as she rushed over to where her father and brother were.

Moira walked up from behind Diana to join her as Tristan watched Vivian go off with embarrassment.

"Puke," Diana muttered.

"I'll catch you later," Moira laughed to her.

"Yeah, I'll catch you later," Diana calmly replied.

The bells of the town hall signaled the turn of the hour into midnight. Diana sighed and turned to Tristan.

"Happy Halloween," Diana said to him.

"Yeah," Tristan replied, "but to be honest, I'm kind of sick of Halloween… no offense."

"No – I'm the same right now," Diana replied. "I kind of just want to go home."

The two of them looked at each other awkwardly as they were left alone atop of the steps.

"Diana?" Tristan asked.

"What?"

"I'm… I'm sorry about what I said to you…"

"No, I should be sorry," Diana replied. "I trapped you in that situation, and that wasn't fair of me to do."

"Are we still friends?" Tristan wondered.

Diana gently laughed, looking away before looking back to Tristan. He held a sincere and apologetic face alongside his green eyes. Diana stepped towards him.

"Kids!" Charlemagne shouted, startling both of them.

"Charles!" Tristan yelled, stepping down and running towards him.

"Where've you been?" Diana asked, rushing forward to join Tristan.

"I've been… working," Charlemagne explained. "I'll tell you the rest as we go home. How are you? Are you both alright? I saw your message, Tristan, but was caught up in jail, and then I had to go to the cemetery, and so on and so forth. I'm just glad you were paying attention and remembered what I said, I suppose, so you could take care of it yourself. Both of you… I'm glad you're both alright."

Charlemagne walked them back to the truck and began to tell them about the last two days in great detail from the escape the research facility to the murder at Medici Manor. He then went on to tell them about the observatory, Barry Lambert, and the theft at Cabernet Laboratories. From there, he told them about his arrest at the police station, and his rescue by Sabrina's grandmother. He then told them about his peace with Cole Phillips and confrontation with Nero Medici.

By the time he had finished his story, it was one o'clock and the children went off to bed. Charlemagne bid them goodnight before retreating to his own room to pass out. The kids went to their respective rooms with Tristan going to his and falling asleep with a smile on his face. Diana combed her hair in the bathroom, pensive and pausing every so often. She gave a calm smile and tied her hair into a ponytail before going to bed and falling asleep.

Epilogue

Charlemagne set his tools onto his dresser and looked at them all. He looked disappointed but cheered up as he sighed. He left his bedroom to go to the bathroom and get ready for bed. When he returned to go to bed, he paused as his ears twitched with the sound of a floorboard creaking. He turned around to look behind him, seeing the door open and a shadowy figure stand under the door frame.

"Mr. Charlemagne de la Cabernet," a female voice said in an elegant Londoner accent.

Charlemagne looked at the silhouette, trying to make out the pale face of the woman in a black blazer and skirt.

"Who are you?" Charlemagne questioned. "How did you get into my house? Are you the mole?"

"I am no mole," the woman replied. "I'm an agent of a secret organization, the name of which you need not know. We monitored the situation in Allabrese tonight, and we were impressed by your actions. However, we were more impressed by your inventions and have interest in them."

"Agent?" Charlemagne questioned. "What is it to you? The crisis is over, no thanks to yourself and your secret society! Something like this will never happen again!"

"That assurance is not good enough for my bosses. We seek a deterrent in case this were to *ever* happen again," the woman said.

"If something like this does ever happen again, I will be there to stop it. I trust myself more than I trust some organization that hid in the shadows when my town needed help. Now if you'd please, get out of my home."

“I’m disappointed by your answer, but not surprise,” the woman said, stepping back in the darkness. “However, Mr. Cabernet. Please know that we will be watching you closely.”

“I’m touched,” Charlemagne remarked.

The woman walked off. Charlemagne waited for a moment before going to the doorway, stepping out and checking the corridor before the foyer to see where the woman went. He shook his head before going back to his bedroom and closing the door behind him.

“I’m probably hallucinating,” Charlemagne sighed, walking over to the French Window to open it and step outside.

A gentle freefall of snow fell from the sky and began to cover the field behind the mansion. Charlemagne looked beyond the garden of the house and towards the Rocky Mountains as they were already capped in their eternal winter blankets. He remained at the balcony for several minutes, silent and pensive before returning inside and closing the door. He went to bed and laid down. With a great big yawn, he turned to his side and closed his tired eyes, hiding them to the light around him. His mind drifted into his own subconsciousness for a rest that he deserved, and peace that would last for now.

"Nothing is more difficult than to realize that every man has a distinct soul, that every one of all the millions who live or have lived, is as whole and independent a being in himself, as if there were no one else in the whole world but he."

– Bl. John Henry Newman

www.ingramcontent.com/pod-product-compliance
Lightning Source LLC
LaVergne TN
LVHW010657110826
845149LV00014B/3136